T0316225

Bello:

hidden talent rediscovered!

Bello is a digital only imprint of Pan Macmillan,
established to breathe new life into previously published,
classic books.

At Bello we believe in the timeless power of the imagination,
of good story, narrative and entertainment and we want to use
digital technology to ensure that many more readers
can enjoy these books into the future.

We publish in ebook and Print on Demand formats
to bring these wonderful books to new audiences.

About Bello:

www.panmacmillan.com/imprints/bello

About the author:

www.panmacmillan.com/author/andrewgarve

Andrew Garve

Andrew Garve is the pen name of Paul Winterton (1908–2001). He was born in Leicester and educated at the Hulme Grammar School, Manchester and Purley County School, Surrey, after which he took a degree in Economics at London University. He was on the staff of *The Economist* for four years, and then worked for fourteen years for the *London News Chronicle* as reporter, leader writer and foreign correspondent. He was assigned to Moscow from 1942–5, where he was also the correspondent of the BBC's Overseas Service.

After the war he turned to full-time writing of detective and adventure novels and produced more than forty-five books. His work was serialized, televised, broadcast, filmed and translated into some twenty languages. He is noted for his varied and unusual backgrounds – which have included Russia, newspaper offices, the West Indies, ocean sailing, the Australian outback, politics, mountaineering and forestry – and for never repeating a plot.

Andrew Garve was a founder member and first joint secretary of the Crime Writers' Association.

Andrew Garve

THE GALLOWAY CASE

First published in 1960 by Collins

This edition published 2012 by Bello
an imprint of Pan Macmillan, a division of Macmillan Publishers Limited
Pan Macmillan, 20 New Wharf Road, London N1 9RR
Basingstoke and Oxford
Associated companies throughout the world

www.panmacmillan.com/imprints/bello
www.curtisbrown.co.uk

ISBN 978-1-4472-2050-3 EPUB
ISBN 978-1-4472-2049-7 POD

Chapter One

The assignment that took me to the Channel Islands, that Thursday before Easter, hardly rated the boat fare by ordinary news standards. I was sent to interview an elderly financier named James Craven, who'd just published his memoirs. The special interest for my paper, the *Post*, was that Craven had written some harsh things about a politician who happened to be in the black books of Lord Eynsford, the *Post's* chairman, and I was to try and get more ammunition for his lordship's vendetta. Ames, the News Editor, gave me my instructions with a more than usually cynical grin, and off I went to Jersey. The interview was straightforward—Craven turned out to be a garrulous old boy who was only too eager to expand his criticisms. I phoned half a column on Thursday evening and Ames, in genial mood, said I needn't come in again till after the Monday holiday.

That suited me fine. I'd never been to the Channel Islands before and knew nothing of Jersey except that it raised cows and early potatoes and was an income-tax refuge for the retired wealthy. The prospect of doing a little exploring was pleasant, especially as the weather was warm. I fixed up at a modest pub in St. Helier, the capital and only town, and settled down to enjoy the rare luxury of four days off in a row.

I spent the next morning looking round St. Helier—idling through the maze of little streets, climbing to the huge fort that dominates the town, inspecting the boats in the harbor, drinking beside the waterfront, and listening, fascinated, to the strange babel of English, French and Anglo-Norman around me. After lunch I took a bus along the coast to one of the wilder corners of the island, called

Corbière Point, which the guidebook said was worth a visit. There was a lighthouse off the Point, set high above a wilderness of weed-covered rocks, and the book said you could walk round it by going out along a paved causeway that was exposed at half tide. When I arrived the causeway was high and dry, with a quiet pool of sapphire water on either side. I crossed to the lighthouse and climbed a lot of steps and spent some time admiring the view from the lower gallery. Then I returned to the Point and stretched out on a slope of moorland turf to smoke a pipe and wait for the afternoon bus back.

Quite a number of people came out to the Point in cars during the next hour or so and most of them walked across to the lighthouse. After a while, though, the spreading pools began to lap at the sides of the causeway and the stream of visitors stopped. The tide must have had a tremendous rise and fall for at one moment the pavement was dry and the next it was under several inches of swirling water. I was thinking the place wouldn't be a very healthy spot for a swim when I saw someone scrambling over the rocks at the foot of the lighthouse. It was a girl, and she was in a great hurry. She reached the end of the causeway, raced along it until she came to the water, and stopped in dismay.

I watched her for a moment, and then went down to see if I could give her any help or advice. The water was surging over the paving stones in a rather offputting way and there were some nasty-looking eddies, but I knew it probably wasn't more than a foot deep in the center. The girl began to take off her shoes and stockings. About thirty yards separated us. A moment later she'd set off along the submerged causeway, holding her skirt up with one hand and clutching a lot of impedimenta with the other. As well as her handbag and shoes she had a straw bag with a thermos and book sticking precariously out of the top and I felt certain she'd drop something. I took off my own shoes and socks and rolled my trousers above the knees and went to meet her. There was a lot of weight in the heaving water but no real danger yet. The girl certainly didn't appear unduly alarmed. She came steadily on, keeping her eyes fixed on the causeway below the surface, and we met near the middle. I took the straw bag from her and helped her over the deepest bit and then led the way back to the shore.

As we reached dry land she gave me a charming smile and said. "That was very kind of you."

I said it was a pleasure. I'd been too occupied with knight errantry to take in any details of her appearance before, but now I had a good look at her. She was worth it. She had the biggest gray eyes I'd ever seen, a beautifully shaped mouth, and thick dark hair that fell smoothly almost to her shoulders. I guessed she was in her middle twenties.

"Cutting it a bit fine, weren't you?" I said.

"Yes—wasn't it stupid?" She squeezed a few drops of water from the bottom of her skirt. "One more minute and I'd have been there for six hours. What a thought!"

"I dare say the lighthouse keeper could have put up with you," I said.

She gave me a quick glance, and smiled again. "I was deep in a book—I wasn't thinking about the time at all. ... You didn't get too wet, I hope?"

I assured her I hadn't.

She parked her things and sat down on the short grass, stretching out her legs to dry them in the sun. She had very nice legs. She had a very nice figure, too.

"Are you on holiday here?" she asked.

"Well, yes and no," I said. "I've got the weekend off, but actually I came to do a job for the *Post*. I'm a reporter."

"*Are* you?" she looked interested. "I see the *Post* occasionally. ..." It was the *Times*, I noticed, that was sticking out of her bag. "Would I know your name?"

"It's Peter Rennie," I said.

"Then I do know it. ... Didn't you write some articles about hooliganism in schools a little while ago?"

"Yes."

"Rather provocative ones!"

I grinned. "That's a nice way of putting it. Some people said they were grossly exaggerated."

"And were they?"

"Not grossly."

She laughed. "They stirred up a lot of controversy, anyhow, judging by the letters I saw. I suppose that was the idea." She was very cool and self-possessed and, to me, enormously attractive. She wasn't wearing a ring, I noticed, and I wondered what was wrong with the men in her part of the world.

After a moment she said, "What have you been doing here—sleuthing?"

"Nothing so exciting," I said. I told her about my interview with the financier, and the reason for it, as she calmly drew on her stockings. The story seemed to amuse her. "What about you?" I asked. "Are you on holiday?"

She gave me a quizzical look. "Yes and no goes for me, too," she said. I waited, but she didn't volunteer any more information.

She had her shoes on, now, but she seemed in no hurry to leave. I asked her if she was catching the bus back to St. Helier, and she said she was. That gave us fifty minutes. I dropped down beside her on the grass and we went on talking and smoking and enjoying the sun. I don't remember now what we talked about—it was all quite superficial—but we got on very well together. She had a natural, friendly manner and I was in the most cheerful spirits myself and the conversation flowed easily. For me the fifty minutes slipped by like five, and I was quite sorry when we had to leave to get the bus.

I learned a little more about her on the way back, but not much. She was staying, she said, at the Paragon, which I knew was one of the most expensive hotels in St. Helier. Apparently she was there on her own. She'd arrived in Jersey the previous day, and she was going back to England next morning. That was disappointing.

It was nearly dusk when we reached St. Helier. Outside the bus, she turned to say good-by. "Thank you again for coming to my rescue!" she said. "And for a pleasant afternoon."

"Thank *you!*" I said, and paused. I didn't at all want to let her go. "Look," I said, "if you're not doing anything special tonight, would you have dinner with me?"

4

She hesitated, smiling.

"Please!" I said. "I might be able to turn you into a regular reader!"

She laughed. "I'd like to very much."

"Then suppose I call for you at your hotel around seven. That'll give us time for a drink before dinner. Okay?"

"Lovely. I shall look forward to it."

"The only thing is, I don't know your name. . . ."

She smiled again. "It's a very ordinary one," she said. "It's Mary Smith."

I called in at the local publicity office to get some advice about a good place to eat, and finally booked a table at the Silver Bay, about four miles outside St. Helier, where they had dancing on weekends. I also fixed up for a self-drive car for the evening. On the dot of seven I drove round to the Paragon and gave my name to the porter. Mary came down in about ten minutes. She'd changed into a slinky black dress and was exquisitely groomed, so that I scarcely recognized the tweedy, wind-blown girl I'd met at Corbière. I restrained an impulse to give a low whistle and just said "My!" She looked pleased, and I steered her to the car.

The Silver Bay turned out to be a spacious modern hotel on the edge of the beach, with a romantic view across the water to the twinkling lights of St. Helier and an atmosphere of great luxury inside. We had a couple of drinks in the bar and went in to dinner just after eight. The dining room was pleasantly full and our table was just the right distance from the band. We studied the menu carefully and settled for lobster cocktails and fried chicken, with a bottle of Château Latour '43 that couldn't have been improved upon.

It was, in all respects, a memorable dinner. Our talk was lighthearted, but more personal than it had been in the afternoon. Mary asked me if I'd always worked on the *Post* and I said no, I'd joined a paper in Norwich after doing my stint in the Army and served an apprenticeship there for three years covering things like police-court proceedings and rate payers' meetings and local flower shows before I'd got my chance in Fleet Street. She asked me what it was like being a reporter on a national newspaper and I gave her a caricature of the life, with all the amusing and bizarre illustrations I could think of, that took us through the lobster. She was a most stimulating audience. She said she'd once tried to get a job on a newspaper herself, just for the experience, in one of the colonies, and from there we got onto travel and it appeared she'd been pretty much everywhere. Apparently she'd been all set to go to the university at nineteen but her father, of whom she spoke with warm affection, had whisked her off on a world trip instead. He sounded like a man of means but she didn't tell me what he did. On the whole, she said, she thought the trip had been more useful to her than the degree in sociology that she'd planned. She was a curious mixture. She had a face and figure that any pin-up girl might have envied, yet she was fundamentally serious—almost an academic type, in fact. I found it an irresistible combination. I probed away delicately and asked her if she lived with her parents, and she said her mother had died when she was a child and though she saw a great deal of her father when he was around he traveled a lot and was very independent and erratic, so she found it more convenient to share a London flat with a girl friend. I asked her if she was an only child and she said she was. It emerged that she was younger than I'd thought, a mere twenty-four. The poise and sophistication had deceived me.

I asked her if she had a job and she said yes, and I asked asked what sort of job.

"I'm a secretary," she said, after a moment.

I remembered what she'd said about her Jersey visit not being entirely a holiday. I said, "Are you being a secretary here?"

"Actually," she said carefully, "I came to see someone."

I grinned. "A man about a dog?"

"Something like that . . ." She gave me her charming smile. "I'm sorry to be so clamlike but—well, I'm supposed to be a *confidential* secretary."

"Okay," I said, "I can take a hint. . . . Would you care to dance?"

"I'd love to dance."

6

She was tall for a woman, but I'm tall for a man so it didn't matter. She danced beautifully, I danced adequately. I had no urge to talk any more. It was wonderful just holding her in my arms. She seemed to find being held quite pleasant. Once we'd started we danced and danced.

It was toward the end of the evening, as we were finishing a slow waltz, that I suddenly said, "Mary, do you have to go back tomorrow?"

"I'm afraid so," she said.

"Not to work, surely?"

"No—not to work."

"A sick relative?"

She laughed and shook her head.

"Your father?"

"No, he's busy this weekend."

"A boy friend?"

"I haven't got a boy friend."

"Now that I find quite incredible."

"I had one, but it didn't work out," she said.

So that was it!

"Then why not stay?" I pressed her. "We could keep the car and explore the island. It would be a lot of fun."

"You're rather impulsive, aren't you?"

"Since I met you, yes."

The music started up and I took her in my arms again without having had a real answer. We danced till the band packed up. Then I drove her back to the Paragon. I kissed her good night and she returned my kiss. There was nothing academic about the way she kissed. Presently she said she must go in. I wanted to ask her for her phone number in London, but first I tried again to persuade her to stay. "It's going to be a wonderful day tomorrow," I said. "I heard the weather forecast—fine and warm. We could go up to the north coast, take our lunch, sun bathe. Anything you like."

She smiled. "You're very persistent."

"But of course. 'Never say die' is my motto. *Please*, Mary . . .!"

She was silent for a moment. Then, to my amazement and delight, she said, "Well, I suppose I could stay one more day. Are you quite sure you want me to?"

"There's nothing in the world I want more."

"Exaggerating again!" she said. "All right—look in after breakfast and perhaps I'll still be here. . . . Good night, Peter! Thank you for a lovely time." She waved, and went into the hotel.

I drove off in a romantic haze. Mary's delicate fragrance still filled the car. I was utterly bewitched. I'd never felt about any girl as I felt about her. I kept saying "Mary Smith" over and over to myself and thinking how lovely it sounded. I'd always liked the name "Mary," but that was only the half of it. I knew I must really have fallen for her because, for the first time in my life, I could see poetry in "Smith" too!

She did stay on next day and—when it came to it—the two following days as well. Every moment with her was an exquisite pleasure for me. I was soon deep in a whirlwind courtship, heady and exhilarating. I had no hesitations, no reservations. I'd fallen in love with her, I wanted her, and I wanted her for keeps. I told her so. She said I couldn't possibly be sure, as we'd only just met. I said common sense might be on her side but time was on mine and I'd prove it to her. She made no avowals herself, but her actions seemed to speak at least as loudly as words. She'd stayed with me from choice. She was gay and happy in my company. She obviously liked me a lot. For the moment, that was good enough for me.

We had a pretty active weekend. On Saturday we took the car and explored the island in gorgeous spring weather, picnicking on a cliff top above an empty beach, with wild daffodils all around us and the scent of gorse in the air. Afterward we walked for miles along the deserted sands and in the evening we went dancing once more. On Sunday we walked again, up one charming valley and down another, making love a little and taking snapshots of each other with a small Kodak I'd brought. That was our day of rest. On Monday Mary suggested we should take a small sailboat out and in next to no time she'd arranged it. I hadn't done much sailing myself but apparently she had—her father, she said, had a boat and they often went out together—and she certainly turned out to be very competent. We had an idyllic day.

I still hadn't discovered where she worked or why she'd come to Jersey. I teased her about it a little, pretending she was deliberately trying to give herself an enticing aura of mystery. She laughed and said there wasn't any mystery, except quite temporarily, and that "later on" she'd tell me all about herself. I was curious, but I didn't want to seem prying, and all I really cared about was that there should be a "later on"—which seemed to be understood. We were going back on the boat together on Tuesday morning, and Mary was going to run me up to town in her car. She'd had to make a call in Hampshire on her way down from London, she said, so she'd driven to Southampton and garaged her car there. She still refused to commit herself about the future in words, but I felt pretty sure everything was going to be all right.

We got back to St. Helier about teatime after our sail and went off to our respective hotels to change. It was our last evening and we were going to dine and dance again. I arranged to call for Mary at half past six. I still had the self-drive car and at twenty past six I drove round to the Paragon and sat down in the lobby to wait for her. She was a bit late coming down and I guessed she was making herself look specially terrific for this last night. I picked up a morning paper that was lying around and glanced through the headlines—I'd got shockingly behindhand with the news while I'd been in Jersey—but it was a thin, holiday paper and I soon put it aside. Presently I became aware that the porter was regarding me rather oddly. He knew me pretty well, of course, by now. After a moment he came over to me.

"You're not waiting for Miss Smith, are you, sir?" he said.

"Yes. Why?"

"She's left."

I stared at him. *"Left!"*

"That's right, sir. She checked out an hour ago. I believe she was catching the six o'clock plane to London."

I continued to gaze at him stupidly. "But that's impossible," I said. "I was to meet her here at six-thirty."

He looked quite concerned himself. "I'm sorry, sir—I'm afraid she's gone, all right. Made up her mind all of a sudden, I s'pose."

"But I was with her till nearly five and she said nothing then about going. . . . Surely she left some message for me?"

"No, sir, not that I know of."

"Didn't she say anything to you?"

"She just asked for her bill at the desk, sir, and said she wanted a taxi to the airport right away, and I called one, and off she went."

"I see. . . ." I stood there for a moment, gazing at him helplessly. "Well, thank you . . ." I turned away, completely dazed. It seemed beyond belief that she could have gone off without getting in touch with me, without even leaving a note. It *was* beyond belief. It occurred to me that she might have dropped a message in at my own pub, which I hadn't received yet, and I hurried back to ask. But there was nothing there.

I went into the bar and ordered a double Scotch and tried to figure things out. If Mary and I had had any sort of quarrel, any misunderstandings or difficulties at all, I could have understood it better—but we hadn't. I couldn't think of a thing in our relationship to account for her abrupt and unexplained flight. We'd parted on the best of terms—on terms of tenderness, in fact. I knew she'd been looking forward to the evening and she'd seemed not to have a care in the world.

I think I felt more baffled than angry at that moment. On the face of it, it was such a discourteous as well as heartless thing to do that I just couldn't accept it at its face value. It seemed so utterly out of character. There must, I told myself, be some good explanation, some overriding reason. But what? Could there be some tie-up, I wondered, between this hurried flight and the extreme caginess Mary had shown about her job and her presence in Jersey? Had something suddenly cropped up in connection with her work?

At that point I went back to the Paragon to make some more inquiries. The porter didn't seem at all surprised to see me again. In fact, he was almost embarrassingly sympathetic.

I said, "Do you know if Miss Smith had any telephone calls after she came in?"

"Definitely not, sir."

"Did she telephone anyone herself?"

"No, sir."

"Are you sure?"

"Positive, sir. If she'd rung from her room it'd have had to go through the switchboard and if she'd used the box down here I'd have seen her."

"Did she go out at all?"

"No, sir."

"Did she have any visitors?"

"No, sir."

That seemed to be that. Whatever had sent her flying off, it didn't look as though it could have been any new development from outside. That made the affair even more inexplicable.

I said, "How did she seem when she went off? Was she agitated?—was she upset?"

"She was a bit pale, sir, I thought—and in a great hurry. That's all."

I nodded. For the moment, my inventive powers had come to an end—but I'd learned enough to settle my own course of action. She'd been pale. Something serious must have happened, even if it was only in her own mind. Perhaps she needed help. Clearly, I must go after her.

It was only then that I realized, with a feeling close to panic, that I knew neither her address nor her telephone number. I snatched up the hotel register and turned to the entries for the previous Thursday. Mary's entry read "Mary Smith, London." There was no address. And even the name "Mary Smith" had suddenly begun to seem unconvincing. I put the register back and asked the receptionist if Miss Smith had reserved her room by phone or letter. The girl said neither, she'd just walked in off the boat and engaged it on the spot. I asked if she'd paid her bill by check or in cash, and the girl said in cash. I was getting nowhere fast.

Then I had another idea. If Mary had left by air, she must have given her full name and address to the airport people for their passenger list. *They* wouldn't have accepted "Mary Smith, London."

I went out to the car and drove straight to the airport. I had a bit of a job wheedling my way into the confidence of the girl clerk in the booking office, but in the end she turned up her records for me—and the information I wanted was there. "Mary Smith, 8 Landon Mews, London, S.W.1." With infinite relief I wrote it down. It wouldn't be long now before I was hearing Mary's explanation from her own lips.

I couldn't get a seat on a plane that night, but I caught the first one out of Jersey next day and by mid-morning I was in a taxi on my way to Landon Mews. I'd no idea whether Mary would be home or not but I was free till evening and could wait all day if necessary. She'd have to come home sometime. I chafed a bit as the taxi got bogged down in a series of traffic blocks, but by twelve-fifteen I was there. I paid off the cab and walked up the Mews with a racing pulse. I passed numbers 1, 2, and 3, and stopped at number 4. I stopped there because that was where the Mews came to an end. There wasn't a number 8. I knocked at the door of number 4 and described Mary to the woman who opened it, just in case there'd been some mistake over the number, but the woman said she didn't know anyone like her. I went to the nearest post office and checked with the London directory to see if there was any other Landon Mews. There wasn't, but there was a Landon Street in S.W.7. I picked up another cab and drove there. Number 8 was a grocer's shop, and they knew nothing of Mary Smith. As a last resort, I tried a Clandon Mews in S.W.3. Then I gave up. It was no use deceiving myself any longer—there'd been no mistake. Mary had deliberately given a false address at Jersey airport, and as I was the only person who was likely to be on her trail she'd clearly done it with me in mind. Taken together with the fact that she'd left no message for me, the conclusion was inescapable. She'd ditched me. For some reason that I couldn't begin to comprehend, she'd decided not to see me again.

Chapter Two

I was on the night turn at the *Post* that night, starting at eight o'clock. Apart from a sensational murder story that the crime man had already been assigned to, there was almost no news about. That suited me well, for I'd never felt less in the mood for work. I stuck my feet on a desk in the Reporters' Room and pretended to be dozing so that I wouldn't be disturbed, and for the next hour or so I concentrated on the problem of Mary's extraordinary behavior.

There were, as far as I could see, two broad possibilities—neither of them very convincing. The first was the obvious one—that she'd simply had a change of heart about me. It would have had to be very sudden, of course, but such things did happen. It might have been connected with that former boy friend she'd mentioned. Perhaps she'd never really got him out of her system. She could have started her affair with me on the rebound, persuaded herself she was fond of me, and then had a sudden emotional *bouleversement* in the Paragon that evening, realized her mistake, and decided to make a clean break. It was feasible—but only just. For one thing, if she'd been as fundamentally unsettled as that I'd have expected to see some sign of instability in her manner. In fact, she'd been calm and relaxed. For another, I still couldn't believe she'd have gone off without a word, however upset she'd been. It would have cost her nothing to scribble a farewell line.

The second possibility, a much more melodramatic one, was that she'd been putting on an act all the time, using me for some secret purpose of her own and discarding me when I was no longer necessary to her. It seemed pretty fantastic, but then so was the way she'd behaved. And what, after all, did I really know about her or her mysterious visit to Jersey? A clever and attractive girl might be mixed up in almost anything, from crime to the intelligence service. Yet Mary wasn't my idea of a modern Mata Hari or a gangster's moll. Even if she had been, I couldn't imagine what possible purpose a romantic affair with me would have served. And wasn't it I who had started the affair and done all the running, not she? In any case, I had an inner conviction that her feelings toward me at the time had been genuine. I could be wrong, but in such matters one went by instinct and that was my instinct.

Still baffled, I turned to the practical question of what I was going to do. In principle I hadn't any doubt about that. If it was humanly possible I was going to find her. It wasn't just that I was head over heels in love with her—her disappearance had become a challenge and my professional blood was up. I'd traced vanished persons for the *Post* before now with very little to go on and I didn't see why I shouldn't be successful on my own account. Not that I underrated the peculiar difficulties in Mary's case. I had the snapshots I'd taken of her in Jersey, which might help, but when I mentally totted up the bits of solid information I had about her I realized they amounted to almost nothing. I knew she was attractive and intelligent; I knew she had taste in clothes and the money to indulge it; I knew she read the *Times* and had traveled; I knew she could dance well; I knew she could sail a boat. That was about all. Everything else was what she'd told me and none of it need be true. I didn't know for certain that she was a secretary or that she lived with a girl friend in London. Even the name she'd given me might not be her real name. Probably it wasn't. I'd already rung the ten Mary Smiths in the London telephone directory as a routine move and none had been the right one. However, there was one clue that seemed to offer possibilities. Whatever Mary had been up to I couldn't see why she should have told me she'd driven down to Southampton and garaged her car there if she hadn't. And if she had, I might well be able to get on its track.

I couldn't do anything about it right away because I was sent off to East Anglia next day on a story. That assignment came to an end on Friday and I had Saturday free. By that time my snapshots of Mary had been developed and I collected them. They'd all come out pretty well and I found them horribly nostalgic. I put them in my pocket and drove straight down to Southampton. Mary had told me her car had been a present from her father but she hadn't said what make it was, so it was a bit like looking for the proverbial needle. I spent all day calling at garages, showing my photographs, and talking to managers and mechanics. I was working through a list I'd compiled from a local directory and there were an awful lot of garages. I'd almost given up hope when, just before six, I suddenly got on the trail. The proprietor of a small garage in a back street near the station recognized Mary from her picture and my description. But that was as far as it went. She'd been driving, he thought, a Morris Ten, but he hadn't any record of its registration number. She'd hired a lock-up for the weekend, he said, and with lockups they didn't bother to make a note of the numbers. It was pretty sickening, because with a bit more luck my search could easily have ended right there. The only crumb of comfort, a small one, was that on this point at least Mary had told the truth.

I didn't have any more days off for a week and could do no more than plan the next move—which would have to be, I decided, a second visit to the Channel Islands. If Mary's business in Jersey had been legitimate and I could trace her contacts there, I ought to be able to get her address. I waited till I had a couple of free days together and then flew back to St. Helier. I spent a grueling twenty-four hours in the town, trying to check Mary's movements on the day she'd arrived. I talked to legions of taxi drivers, bus conductors, shopkeepers and policemen. I must have shown her picture to hundreds of people. Some of them thought they remembered seeing her around but they were all pretty vague. The key period seemed to have been the Thursday afternoon, more or less the same time that I'd been interviewing my financier. Apparently she'd left the Paragon at about three o'clock, on foot, and had got back there about five. But where she'd been in those two hours remained a mystery. She'd seen someone, who might still be on the island, but there were fifty thousand inhabitants and I couldn't interview them all. What I did do was call at the office of the local paper to see if I could get one of my snapshots reproduced as an advertisement. It turned out the quality wasn't good enough but I did the next best thing and inserted a few carefully worded lines in the personal column seeking information about Mary Smith's visit and address. Then I flew back to London. As far as Jersey was concerned I'd shot my bolt.

When no replies came to my advertisement I seriously considered abandoning the search. I'd done all the straightforward things and any further inquiries were bound to be arduous. I told myself I was behaving like a damned fool, that the world was full of attractive and interesting women, that my feelings for Mary couldn't have any real depth when I'd only known her for three days, and that if I made an effort I could soon put her out of my mind. But it didn't work. You can't argue yourself out of being in love. I tried taking out other girls I knew, charming girls, and it was pleasant enough but the spark was lacking. For me, Mary was unique. I didn't *want* to put her out of my mind. I wanted to find her. I began to consider new lines of inquiry. There was the secretarial end, of course—though with confidential secretaries almost as common in London as pigeons it was difficult to know where to start looking. I'd probably be just as likely to find her by camping out in Piccadilly Circus Underground, where everyone was supposed to show up sooner or later. Still, I did try the larger agencies. When I drew a blank there I switched to the boat aspect—Mary might, I thought, have belonged to some yacht club. I called on most of the clubs in and around London but again I had no success.

So far I hadn't told anyone in the office what I was up to, but one night on the late turn when I was feeling pretty desperate and very much in need of a fresh view, I told the whole story to a friend and colleague named Harry Shawcross who was also a very shrewd reporter. He was amused, naturally, and extremely intrigued—and, as it turned out, helpful. He said, with a grin, "Have you tried the telephone directory?" I said I'd tried the Mary Smiths, but I hadn't gone any further into the Smiths because I didn't believe that was her real name anyway.

He said, "Well, I don't know about that, old boy—I'd have thought it probably *was* her real name."

"Why?"

"Well, for one thing, if it was assumed I can't see her drawing attention to its ordinariness the way she did when she told you what it was. . . . Anyhow, it was what she wrote in the hotel register, wasn't it? And that was before she met you—before there was any question of deceiving you."

"She could have been deceiving others."

Harry shook his head. "If her business in Jersey was so secret that she needed to give a false name, I'd have thought she'd have been a bit more inventive. Mary Smith's so commonplace it sticks out like a sore thumb. And wouldn't she have added some address, the way she did at the airport? A phony address would have been much less conspicuous in the book than none at all. I may be wrong, old boy, but 'Mary Smith, London' sounds to me like the genuine entry of someone with nothing to hide. If I were you I'd get on the blower again."

I wasn't convinced, but I was impressed. I picked up the last volume of the London directory and paged through the Smiths. There were over a hundred columns of them—seven thousand entries, at a rough guess. Seven years for Rachel seemed modest by comparison! But only a small proportion would be "possibles"—those where one of the initials was M. It was worth a try. I took a pencil and worked my way through the whole seven thousand, ticking the "possibles." There were 276 Smiths with one of their initials M. I divided them into the more likely and the less likely. Mary, I thought, as a sophisticated business girl in no apparent need of money, would have chosen to live near Central London rather than in some out-of-the-way place on the fringe. The Post Office zoned its numbers according to distance from Oxford Circus so it was easy to sort them out. I drew up three lists. There were 66 entries within five miles of Oxford Circus, 143 in the next belt, and 67 in an outer belt.

During the next few days, my work at the office was scarcely more than a diversion from the serious business of getting in touch with Smiths. I ducked jobs shamelessly in order to have more time free. I needed all the time I could get because I often had to ring numbers more than once and sometimes, when I couldn't get a reply at all, there was nothing for it but to visit the house and check with the neighbors. It was a long job, but I plugged away and by the end of a week or so I'd finished the first list of entries.

Then, willy nilly, I had to break off the search. The I.R.A. had suddenly become very active in Ulster, attacking police stations and blowing up buildings, and in the middle of June I was sent off to Ireland to cover the story. It was a satisfying assignment, the more so because the *Post* decided to go into the situation in a big way and asked for a lot of background material. I was in Eire and Northern Ireland through the rest of June and most of July, buried for much of the time in the wilds of the lovely border country.

I'd stopped looking at Mary's picture by now. I'd looked at all the snaps so often they no longer lived for me. I preferred to imagine her as I'd known her, during those few unbelievably carefree days in Jersey. Everything about her was as vividly fresh in my memory as the day we'd parted. I still had an almost unbearable ache for her. I still worried about her. I often wondered what she was doing, what she was thinking. It was hard to believe I wasn't sometimes in her thoughts. I still found the whole business quite incredible. The unsolved mystery nagged at me constantly. She'd left a mark on me that would never fade. I knew that. I tried not to dwell morbidly, but it wasn't easy.

It was late in July when I got back to London. I searched eagerly through my accumulated mail, for I hadn't entirely lost the hope that Mary herself would one day try to get in touch with me again. But there was nothing. The lists of telephone numbers were still on my desk at the flat, with 210 numbers still unrung. I flung them into a wastebasket and went to the office. The news front was dead and there was absolutely nothing doing. I thought about Mary all day. When I got home I retrieved the lists and next day I started telephoning again.

It was the intermediate list, now—143 entries. I did a stint each morning. I was rarely on duty at the *Post* before two in the afternoon and often much later so that gave me time to drive out to places like Stanmore and Lee Green and Streatham to check on "no replies," which were much more frequent now because it was the holiday season. By the beginning of August I'd nearly worked through the second batch. Then, suddenly, I picked up a scent.

I'd driven out to a place at Richmond that I'd telephoned on two successive mornings and three successive evenings without getting a reply. The name in the book was M. R. Smith, and the address 14B Weedon Court. By now these visits had become a completely routine affair, and as I turned into an extremely lush block of flats near the river I couldn't have felt less expectant. A uniformed commissionaire was sitting behind a table in the lobby, reading a newspaper. I said I understood there was an M. R. Smith living at 14B and did he happen to know if it was a Miss Mary Smith. He said there wasn't anyone named Smith living there now but there *had* been a Miss Mary Smith. I whisked out my snapshots and he took one look and said, "That's right, that's her."

I could have fallen on his neck. Eagerly I begged him to tell me more. He said that Miss Smith had given up the flat about three months ago. I asked him if he knew where she'd moved to and he said he didn't. I said what about her mail and he said she'd come back twice to collect it and after that there hadn't been any. I said I understood she'd shared her flat with a girl friend and he said, yes, but the girl friend, a Miss Bronson, had got married and he thought that was why Miss Smith had left, because the flats were expensive for a single woman on her own. I asked him if he knew where Miss Bronson had gone and he said, yes, she'd gone to Canada. He didn't know either her married name or her address.

The promising trail seemed to have run into the sand, but I wasn't too worried. The telephone people, I thought, would be able to give me the number that M. R. Smith of Weedon Court had transferred to and that would be all I needed. I found a call box and talked to "Inquiries" and after a short delay they told me they'd no record of a transfer to an M. R. Smith in recent months.

Frustrated, I returned to the commissionaire. I crackled a pound note between my fingers and asked him if there'd been any letters from Miss Smith after she'd left the flat, perhaps returning a key or settling a last bill. He said all correspondence of that sort would be at the head office and anyway he didn't think it was likely because all settling up was done beforehand. I asked him if by any chance he knew where she'd worked and he said all he knew was that she'd been someone's secretary and had often gone off in the mornings to the House of Commons.

The House of Commons! *Of course!* Now that I'd been told I could have kicked myself for not thinking of it before. It fitted Mary perfectly. The knowledge of affairs, the sophistication, the discretion, even the reading of the *Times*—it all added up to the political secretary. Excitement rose in me again. I thrust the pound note into the commissionaire's hand and rushed out to the car and drove at top speed to Westminster. One of the policemen on duty at the House would be sure to know Mary if she was a regular visitor—it was their job to remember every face. The House was in recess, but work must be going on still and I'd probably be able to find someone who could tell me about her. I parked the car near the main entrance and went across to the policeman at the door. I produced my snapshots and explained rather breathlessly that they were of a Miss Mary Smith, whom I believed to be a secretary at the House, and asked him if he could tell me whose secretary she was. I was a bit pressing, especially when I saw from his expression that he'd recognized Mary, and he looked at me suspiciously. Instead of telling me right away he became maddeningly slow and official and asked me who I was and why I was interested and I had to show my press card and go into a lot of personal explanations before he was willing to talk. Then he became quite friendly. He said the lady in the picture *had* worked for Sir Horace Dimmock, who'd been the Secretary of State for the Colonies, but after Sir Horace had resigned his post and his seat a few months back on account of ill health, Miss Smith hadn't been to the House any more and he'd no idea what had happened to her.

I thanked him and made for a phone box and looked up Dimmock's number. It wasn't in the book. Either he had an ex-directory number or he lived in the country, or both. I drove to the office to see if the library could help. There was an envelope full of Dimmock's cuttings and about the first thing I came across was a reference to his constituency—South Hampshire. That, I remembered, was where Mary had stopped on her way to Southampton by car. Another piece had fallen into place. The next cutting was a gossip paragraph dated about a week after Easter saying that Sir Horace Dimmock, whose surprise resignation from the government had been announced the previous day, was planning to give up his Surrey home and settle in Jersey. I continued to riffle through the papers and presently found another paragraph, dated June, saying that Sir Horace had bought a house in Jersey on the outskirts of St. Helier and that he and Lady Dimmock would be moving in at once.

I could probably have got hold of his telephone number in Jersey but I didn't think he'd be likely to give information about his secretary to a stranger over the phone. That evening I wrote him a letter, introducing myself and saying there was something I wanted to ask him that concerned me personally and that I was coming to Jersey in a day or two and would be most grateful if he could see me for a few minutes. Then I booked a seat on a plane for my first free day, a Saturday, and a couple of mornings later I flew to Jersey again. It was about noon when I reached the Dimmocks' house, a pleasant villa overlooking the sea not very far from the Silver Bay. A maid opened the door and I asked her to give Sir Horace my name. She said Sir Horace was ill but she'd tell Lady Dimmock. A moment later I was asked in.

Lady Dimmock was white-haired, gentle and charming. When I told her who I was she remembered my letter. She said she was sorry her husband wasn't well enough to see me and was there anything she could do? I said I thought perhaps there was and told her that I'd met a Mary Smith in Jersey at Easter who I understood had been Sir Horace's secretary. She nodded and said, yes, Mary *had* been one of her husband's secretaries and if I'd met her at Easter that would have been when they'd got her to come to Jersey and take a preliminary look at a house for them, because they themselves had been in the south of France when the agent's particulars had arrived. I said, oh, was *that* it?—I'd wondered what Mary had been doing in Jersey, because although we'd got on very well together she'd been most secretive about the reason for her trip. Lady Dimmock smiled and said she could understand that, because if it had become known that the Colonial Secretary was planning to settle in Jersey, it would have been as good as announcing his resignation from the government and no secretary would have wanted to do that. I said of course not and moved on to my personal problem. I explained that I'd hoped to meet Mary again but that she'd left Jersey without giving me her address and although I'd made some progress in tracing her to her old address it now appeared that she'd moved, and did Lady Dimmock by any chance know her new one? It was a trivial thing to trouble her about, I said, but it was rather important to me. She smiled again and said she'd go and look—she thought Mary *had* written once from a new address, enclosing some papers which she'd overlooked when she'd left Sir Horace rather suddenly after Easter. She went and looked and after a few moments she came back with a letter. She said she'd found the address, but she wasn't absolutely sure she ought to give it to me without Mary's permission. I pretty well went down on my knees to her then. I said I'd fallen in love with Mary and wanted to marry her, but that a misunderstanding had arisen between us which I could hope to clear up only if I saw her again, and if her permission was asked she might not be willing to see me and then I might never get the chance to set things right. Lady Dimmock looked at me appraisingly for a moment and then said that in the circumstances she thought perhaps no harm would be done, and gave me the address. It was Flat 2, Oaklands, Ham Green Road, Kew.

I flew back to London that afternoon with pretty mixed feelings. It was true I'd got all the information I'd come for, and more. It was true that many things which had been a mystery before had been very simply explained. I knew just what Mary had been up to and why she hadn't wanted to tell me whose secretary she was or identify herself too closely to a newspaperman. But the explanation had thrown no new light on her abrupt departure. She had not, it now appeared, been caught up in any dangerous tangle or melodramatic situation which might have accounted for her sudden decision. Perhaps, after all, the most obvious answer was the right one—that she'd simply changed her mind about me and ruthlessly written me off. Perhaps I should have had less belief in her and more humility. Anyway, there wasn't much point in starting to speculate again at this stage. Soon, I'd *know*. And if I didn't like the explanation, at least the long, distracting search would be over.

Once back in London, I wasted no time. I picked up my car and drove straight off to Kew. I got there just before nine. Ham Green Road was an avenue of large, old-fashioned, three-story houses, very different from Weedon Court, but tree-lined and pleasant enough in the summer dusk. I soon found Oaklands. There were three flats, and three bells, and Mary's name was over the middle one. I rang it twice and waited tensely. After a moment I heard footsteps on the stairs. Then the door opened and Mary was standing there.

Chapter Three

For a second or two she just stood there, holding the door and looking at me, her eyes enormous with surprise. Then, in a scarcely audible voice, she said, *"Peter!"* There was alarm in her tone as well as surprise—and yet, it seemed to me a kind of relief, too.

It must have been a difficult moment for her. It was certainly difficult for me. I'd worked for this reunion, if you could call it that, for four long months, and now it had come I was suddenly at a loss for words. There was so much to ask and to say, I didn't know where to begin. And anyway, I could scarcely breathe I was so moved. I said, "Hullo, Mary . . ." and stopped.

For a moment she didn't seem to know what to do. Then she said, "You'd better come up, I suppose," and she turned and led the way up a dimly lit flight of stairs to a little sitting room. The light was better there and I was able to take a closer look at her. She was thinner, and she looked as though she'd been missing a lot of sleep, but somehow it suited her. She seemed to have an added distinction.

She stood away from me, strained and guarded. "So you found me," she said.

"Yes—I found you."

"How did you manage it?"

"Perseverance," I said. "'Never say die'—remember? It would take me a week to tell you all the moves."

"You shouldn't have done it, Peter. You don't imagine I went off like that without a very good reason?"

"I don't know why you went off—but I certainly hope you'll tell me. I used to be an interested party!"

"I would so much rather not."

"Now that I'm here you haven't much choice, have you?"

"It would be much better if you just went away again. Honestly, Peter. For your sake *and* mine."

"Not a hope," I said, and sat down.

She reached for a cigarette and lit it. Her hand was shaking. "I suppose it hasn't occurred to you," she said, "that I might find you—intrusive?"

"Naturally it's occurred to me. If that's how it turns out I'll push off right away—don't worry. But it's taken me four months to find you and I'm certainly not going to leave now without an explanation. Don't you think I'm entitled to one?"

"It's not a question of being entitled. When you know the truth you'll wish you hadn't heard it."

I'll take a chance on that."

She gave a little shrug. "Well, you've asked for it," she said in a flat voice, "so here it is. It's really very simple. . . . When I went back to the Paragon that last afternoon I picked up a paper in the lobby—and I read that my father had been arrested for murder."

I stared at her incredulously.

"So naturally I left at once. . . . The trial came on a month ago. My father was found guilty and condemned to death."

"Mary!"

"He was reprieved last week—but only because they're not hanging people now. He'll probably be in prison for the rest of his life. And that's all."

I was utterly appalled. Questions jostled in my mind, but I was so overcome with the horror of her situation that for a moment I couldn't even speak.

"You must have read about it," Mary went on. "Daddy's real name is Francis Smith, but you'll have known of him as John Galloway, the writer."

"Galloway . . .! Your father's John Galloway?"

"Yes," she said.

"Oh, my God . . .!"

I remembered the case only too well—the outlines of it, at

least—for it had been a sensational one. Galloway, a famous and highly paid author of crime and adventure stories, had filched a plot in a most contemptible way from some wretched little amateur who'd fancied himself as a writer. The man had made trouble, and Galloway had murdered him. That was the gist of it. I was hazy about the details because I'd been in Eire when the case had been hitting the headlines, and since I'd got back I'd been too busy chasing Smiths of every description to catch up with old stuff. But I knew enough.

I said, "God, Mary, I'm so sorry."

"Thank you."

"You must have had a hell of a time."

"That's an understatement," she said wanly.

Silence fell between us like a curtain. In my wildest imaginings I'd never imagined anything as bad as this. My mind was in a ferment and I groped in vain for adequate words. I remembered how warmly she'd always spoken of her father and my heart ached for her. I wanted terribly to do something for her, but I didn't know what.

At last I said, "I can understand now your rushing off as you did—but why on earth didn't you let me know afterward?"

She gave a wry little smile. "Put yourself in my place for a moment. Would *you* have?"

I thought about it, and I knew I wouldn't. I'd have done exactly as she'd done.

I said, "What are you doing about yourself, anyway—are you living here alone?"

"Yes."

"Is that a good idea?"

"I prefer it that way."

"It's a bit of a change from Weedon Court."

"Oh, you went there, did you? Yes, it is, but it's much cheaper. That's why I came, of course. Daddy used to subsidize me, but that's finished now—the defense was very expensive, and there are some big debts. Not mine—I'm all right."

"Do you have a job?"

"Not at the moment, but I'll have to start looking for one soon."

"What about your friends?"

"Oh, they've all been very kind. Most sympathetic!"

"Do you see them?"

"Not often ... I'll probably make some new ones in time."

"I suppose you see your father?"

"Yes, I see him—after a fashion. There's always a partition between us. Part of it's glass, part of it's a grille. I can either see him or hear him, but not both at once. It's not exactly cozy."

"Where is he, Mary?"

"He's in Wandsworth at the moment, but I think he may be moved soon."

"I see." There was another strained pause. Then I said, "Nobody seems to have known you were connected with the case. No one I've met, anyway. I saw Lady Dimmock, you know. She obviously had no idea."

"No, she wouldn't have. I never told them my father was John Galloway. It just didn't arise."

"And you didn't have to give evidence?"

"No—I didn't really know anything. I desperately wanted to speak up for Daddy, but the lawyers said there was absolutely nothing I could say that would do any good and Daddy begged me to keep out of it—he was much more worried about the effect on me than he was about himself. So I stayed in the background."

I nodded, and silence fell again. It was difficult to talk to her, impossible to get to grips with her. She'd been living with her tragedy for a long time and she seemed to have grown a hard, protective shell.

After a moment she said, "Well, there it is, Peter—you know everything now. I'm sorry we had to break things up. You must have had a bad time, too. I often thought about you. It was nice of you to come in search of me. ... And now I really think you'd better go."

"Why must I go?"

"Because it'll be easier for both of us that way."

"But, Mary," I said, "I don't want to leave you—I've only just found you again. Don't you understand, I love you. Please, darling, try and thaw out a bit. What your father's done doesn't affect us—it doesn't alter our feelings for each other. It hasn't altered mine, anyway."

"It will when you've had time to think about it. I've had time. ... It's no good, Peter—we've got to be realistic. That's all over and finished with—it was a different existence."

"I don't accept that, Mary, not for a moment. I love you. I want to look after you. I want to help you."

"There's only one way anyone can help me," she said, "and that's to prove that my father didn't do this thing. And no one will try to do that because no one believes it."

It was an angle that hadn't even occurred to me. From what I remembered of the case it had been an open-and-shut affair.

I said, "Do *you* believe he didn't do it?"

"I'm sure he didn't do it," she said.

"Why?"

"I just know."

I looked at her, rather hopelessly. There never had been, I supposed, a murderer whom some devoted friend or relative hadn't believed in.

There was a framed photograph on a table near the window. I said, "Is that your father?" and Mary nodded. I went over and had a look at it. It showed a man of about fifty, silvering at the temples, with a lively, sensitive face, a humorous mouth, a determined chin. It was an interesting face, a distinguished face, a face full of life and character—but none of that meant much. A murderer didn't have to look like a thug.

I put the photograph down. "Well," I said, feeling my way delicately, "I was out of the country all through the trial—I really know too little about the case to have a view. ...." I met her cold, level gaze and I knew that I'd got to have a view. It wouldn't be her view, I felt sure, but it would be something. "I'll read it up," I said.

"Yes, read it up. And there's no need to study my feelings. Don't think you have to come back, if you find you'd rather not. I shan't expect you and I still think it would be better if you didn't."

"At least," I said, "you won't disappear again?"

"No, I won't do that," she said, softening a little.

"Can I ring you?—I couldn't find a number for you here."

"The telephone's in my landlady's name. It's down in the hall but I can use it. Ring if you want to."

She came downstairs with me. I made a note of the phone number. I tried to think of some parting word of comfort that wouldn't sound trite but I couldn't. She said, "Good night, Peter," in a politely distant voice and I left almost like a stranger.

Chapter Four

I went straight along to the office. As it was Saturday night the building was empty except for the commissionaire at the front box and a solitary reporter on the News Desk. Conditions were just right for a bit of quiet research. I went up to the library, switched on the lights and nosed about in the metal filing cabinets till I found the cuttings of the Galloway case. There was a huge bagful of them, clipped from a dozen different newspapers. The court proceedings had been covered for the *Post* by a man named Wilson, an elderly reporter who always did a very thorough job, and I sorted out his pieces to read first. There were columns and columns of stuff, starting with the usual description of the Old Bailey scene and a pen picture of the prisoner in the dock and then taking in the speeches and evidence almost verbatim. I lit my pipe and began to read the Attorney General's opening for the prosecution. It was factual and restrained and went as follows:

At about eight o'clock last Easter Sunday morning the fully clothed body of a man was found by a lock keeper floating in the River Thames above Teddington Lock. It was subsequently identified as that of Robert Shaw, aged 35, of 12A, Cavendish Road, South Croydon, a librarian employed at a public library in Streatham. There was a severe wound at the back of the head and the skull was later found to be fractured. Death, it was established, had resulted from drowning during unconsciousness and had occurred some twelve hours earlier. The police examined the banks of the river upstream, and about halfway between Teddington and the next town,

Kingston, they found a pair of spectacles beside the towpath which were later identified as Shaw's. One of the lenses was broken. The ground was too hard to have taken any clear footprints at this point but there were signs of trampling in the grass at the edge of the bank consistent with a man having been assaulted there and knocked into the river.

Following the broadcast of a news item in the one o'clock bulletin that day, a man and a girl who lived in the district—Donald Thorpe and Anita Robinson—called at Kingston police station with information. They stated that between eight and nine o'clock on the previous evening they had been walking along the towpath between Kingston and Teddington when they had overheard two men engaging in a violent quarrel aboard a boat tied up at the bank on the tow-path side of the river about three hundred yards above Teddington Lock. The police had already noticed this boat, an auxiliary motor yacht named *Aurora*. It was lying about two hundred yards below the point where Shaw had apparently been attacked and when seen by the police was unoccupied and locked. They proceeded to identify the owner as Francis Noel Smith, a man known to a wide public as the author John Galloway, who is now the prisoner in the dock. Later that day they called on Smith at his flat in London and interviewed him. In reply to questions he admitted that he knew Shaw and that Shaw had visited him on his boat the previous evening and that there had been a quarrel, but he said he knew nothing at all about Shaw's death. He appeared surprised and very worried at the news. He said he would like to write out a complete statement covering his relations with the dead man, and after being cautioned he did so. He was subsequently charged with the murder of Robert Shaw. . . .

I broke off there to have a look at the picture of Shaw that appeared higher up on the page. It showed a rather studious type of man, with a high, prematurely-balding forehead and old-fashioned horn-rimmed glasses with circular lenses that gave him an owl-like appearance. I was about to switch back to the Attorney General when my eye was caught by a headline in an earlier cutting—"Galloway's Own Story"—and I decided to read Galloway's statement first. It was as follows:

My first contact with Robert Shaw occurred about the middle of February last year. I'd just got back from the Canary Islands, where I'd been holidaying for a month between books. There was a lot of accumulated correspondence waiting for me at my flat, including a package from this man Shaw, who was a stranger to me. It contained the typed manuscript of a book-length story—*The Great Adventure*, by Robert Shaw—tied up with pink ribbon. Tucked under the ribbon there was a covering letter. The letter said that Shaw had always been an admirer of my work and that his greatest ambition was to write successfully himself and that he thought he had quite a lot of talent and he'd done a number of short crime stories which he hadn't actually managed to get into print yet, but still hoped to find a home for, and meanwhile he'd written a full-length adventure story and he'd be grateful if I'd read it and let him have a detailed criticism. I didn't much care for the tone of his letter, and as I was anxious to start work myself on a new story that I'd thought up during my voyage back from the Canaries I returned his manuscript to him without opening it, saying I was very sorry but I was too busy to read it.

I heard no more from Shaw for over a year. I spent the next few months writing my story. The idea of it was based on an actual happening reported in the newspapers about twelve months earlier, when two large liners had collided and one had sunk and there'd been talk about trying to recover the sunken liner's automatic course indicator from a depth of 250 feet in an effort to establish responsibility for the disaster. In my story, a bunch of crook divers attempted to recover the indicator first, with the aim of exploiting it financially according to what it revealed. It was a fast-moving story with a lot of action and it turned out very well. It was bought by an American film company before publication for £8,000 and was published in England last January under the title *Full Fathom Forty*.

It was toward the end of March that I had another letter from Shaw. At first I could scarcely remember who he was. His letter said that he'd just finished reading my new novel *Full Fathom Forty* and had been astonished at the extraordinary similarity between my plot and the plot of his own unpublished story *The Great Adventure*, the manuscript of which he'd sent me a year ago. He would very much welcome, he said, an opportunity to meet me and discuss the matter.

I didn't like the sound of that at all. Minor similarities between plots can occur very easily and they can lead to a lot of unpleasantness. It was the more worrying because I hadn't the slightest idea what was actually in his manuscript. Anyway, I asked him to come and see me at my flat and to bring a copy of the manuscript with him.

As soon as he arrived I took a quick look through it. Even a superficial glance was enough to tell me there were indeed some remarkable likenesses in the two plots, though the names of places and characters and ships were all different. I asked him where he'd got his plot from and he said the main idea had come from the newspaper story that everyone had read and that he'd then done a lot of research and reading on the technical aspects and had gradually worked the plot up. I said it was an astonishing coincidence that we'd both worked it up along such similar lines. He said he supposed it *was* a coincidence. I said sharply that it couldn't be anything else. He said the only other explanation he could think of was that, having paged through his manuscript a year ago, I might—quite unconsciously, of course—have absorbed something of his plot and made use of it myself. I told him I hadn't looked at his manuscript—that I hadn't even untied the ribbon. He said my memory must be at fault about that because the manuscript had come back to him with the ribbon tied in quite a different way from the way he'd tied it, so obviously someone had looked at it. I knew then that I was in for trouble. I wasn't at all surprised when he went on to suggest that in the circumstances and considering how lucrative the plot had been—apparently he'd read about the film sale in a trade paper—some financial compensation was due to him. I said that was out of the question. I said I'd like to have a closer look at his manuscript and he agreed to leave it with me.

After he'd gone I read it right through and I was horrified. It was very badly written and as it stood it was quite unpublishable—but the story was the same as mine. Four or five separate incidents, as well as the general structure of the plot, were almost identical. It was hard to believe any longer that the similarity was just a coincidence. The alternative seemed to be that Shaw was a crook.

By now I was too worried to do any serious work and I thought I might as well go and stay on my boat and get on with some fitting-out jobs I was doing, until the situation had cleared up. Meanwhile I telephoned Shaw and asked him to come and see me again, this time at the boat. When he arrived I took the offensive. I said how did I know this manuscript he'd shown me was the same one he'd sent me a year earlier? How did I know he hadn't typed it out after the publication of my story *Full Fathom Forty*, taking my plot and changing all the names and putting it into his own words? He looked very hurt at that and said there were plenty of people who could vouch for the fact that this was his original story, because he'd talked about it and shown it to them directly he'd got it back from me the previous year. He said did I know a thriller writer named Arthur Blundell, and I said of course I did, only he wouldn't be of much help as a witness because he'd died a week or two ago—I'd seen his obituary in the paper. Show said that was true, but he'd been alive when he (Shaw) had sent the manuscript to him nearly a year ago, and he'd read the manuscript and sent a letter about it which Shaw would be happy to show me. I asked him if he'd got the letter with him and he said, no, it hadn't occurred to him that I'd take this line, but he'd bring it for me to see.

He brought it along the next evening. It said that Blundell had read Shaw's manuscript *The Great Adventure* with considerable interest. Blundell thought the plot was absolutely first class, the underwater incidents full of promise, and the description of the *Shomura* (the name Shaw had given to one of the two liners) as she lay on the bottom quite well done—but the writing as a whole was far below publishable standard. He recommended complete rewriting in a much tauter style. It was a very fair criticism and good advice. The letter was dated April 14 of the previous year—a good nine months before my own book had seen the light of day and well before the story had taken final shape even in my own mind. It proved conclusively that Shaw had not copied my book.

I offered him my apologies and said I'd like to think the whole matter over. By now I was very worried indeed. Against all common sense I could only conclude that the duplication of the two plots *had* been a coincidence after all. There was no other possible explanation. But I thought it most unlikely that people would believe that. They'd be much more likely to believe that I'd opened Shaw's manuscript when he'd first sent it, and stolen his plot—and there was only my word for it that I hadn't. I decided that things had become much too serious for me to handle any longer on my own. That night I wrote to Shaw and said that in the circumstances I was putting the whole matter in the hands of my solicitors.

The next evening, Easter Saturday, he called on me unexpectedly at the boat at about eight o'clock. His attitude was a good deal more unpleasant this time. He said there was no point in my wasting a lot of good money going to law and that I wouldn't have a chance as any jury would be bound to decide that I'd stolen his plot. What was more, the American film company that had bought the story might well demand the return of its money when they found that the ownership was in dispute. In short, it would be much wiser and cheaper for me to settle the whole thing for half the film money, namely, £4,000. If I didn't, he said, he would write to my publishers and the Society of Authors and the British Mystery Writers' Guild and tell the whole story. I lost my temper, then, and told him to go to hell and practically threw him off the boat. It was about nine o'clock. He went off along the towpath toward Kingston and I didn't see him again. Half an hour later I also left for Kingston. I picked up my car there and drove back to my flat. That is all I know.

I sat back, wondering grimly if Galloway had consulted his lawyer before making that fascinating statement, and very much doubting it. I had the impression he'd been much more concerned to get his version down quickly than to seek advice. It was a very plausible statement, of course, even engagingly frank, but he'd made a lot of extremely damaging admissions in the course of it and I couldn't help feeling they must have weighed heavily against him with the jury.

I relit my pipe and turned again to the prosecution case. The Attorney General had gone back now to what he called "the beginning of things." The first point he brought out concerned a television appearance that Galloway had apparently made just before his departure for the Canaries. It had been a five-minute interview during which Galloway had given his views on the future of the thriller, described his habits of work, been encouraged to puff the book he'd just finished, and confessed rather ruefully that he hadn't an idea in his head for the next one. Most authors dried up from time to time, he'd said, and that was the position he seemed to have reached. The interviewer had said brightly that perhaps some member of the public would write in and suggest something and Galloway had said heaven forbid and the interview had ended.

Next, the prosecution moved on to Galloway's financial position at that time. It might have been thought, the Attorney General said, that in view of the large and steady sales that Galloway's work had enjoyed for years on both sides of the Atlantic, not to mention frequent serial and film sales, he would have been a rich man—but this was far from being the case. Though his earnings had been high, his expenditures—which included the rent of a service flat in the West End, the purchase and upkeep of a fine boat, and a large outlay on ambitious holidays—had been extravagantly high, too. In addition, some heavy incometax arrears had begun to catch up with him and he'd been in need of some £7,000 to clear his debts to the Inland Revenue and the Special Commissioners, who had become pressing.

In short, the Attorney General said, the position at the time of his departure for the Canaries had been that he owed a great deal of money which he couldn't hope to pay unless he secured another big film sale, and to be sure of doing that he'd needed an exceptionally good plot, which he hadn't got.

The contention of the prosecution was that Galloway had returned from the Canaries still without a good idea. He'd found Robert Shaw's manuscript on his desk, and read it, and decided that though the story was badly written, the plot was first class. And he'd stolen the plot. Obviously there'd been risks, but he'd been in a tight spot and he'd gambled on getting away with it. He'd scrapped the verbiage of the aspiring amateur, Shaw, and substituted his own terse narrative. A point that wouldn't be lost on the jury was that Galloway had kept Shaw's manuscript for almost three weeks. If he hadn't been using it—if, as he'd said, he hadn't even opened it—why had he kept it so long?

The gamble, as it turned out, had failed. Shaw had discovered the plagiarism and had made a fuss. In that connection, the jury must be on their guard against accepting the unsympathetic and one-sided picture of Shaw contained in Galloway's statement. Shaw had not been a very gifted writer, but his painstaking efforts to achieve success in a sphere that had probably been beyond him had certainly not been unworthy. His indignation at having had what was possibly the one really good story idea of his life stolen from him by a man who had already reached the top of the tree had been very natural. Shaw, too, had put his attitude on record, in an unfinished statement apparently intended for his solicitor which had been found in his typewriter after his death. The statement was being introduced in evidence. It showed that Shaw felt himself to be a deeply injured man, fully entitled to the compensation he had claimed. It was possible, though not certain, that he had pressed his claim in an improper way, but the jury would hardly need to be reminded that unwise threats were no excuse for murder.

When Shaw had produced the note from Arthur Blundell confirming his claim, Galloway had realized, belatedly, the full danger of his position. If he allowed the facts to come out, he stood to lose not only a large amount of money but his reputation as a writer of integrity and probably his livelihood. If he didn't, he was faced with a demand for compensation which he couldn't afford to meet. So, the prosecution maintained, after the quarrel on that Easter Saturday evening, when it had become clear that Shaw was adamant for his rights, Galloway had followed him along the dark towpath and struck him from behind and knocked him unconscious into the river to drown. He had chosen to follow him, no doubt, in order to avoid making any incriminating marks on or near the boat itself. The actual assault would have presented no difficulties, for Galloway was an active, muscular man, and Shaw had been a small man, of very poor physique. heavy, round-headed object, probably a hammer. A hammer with a head of the right size had in fact been found in difficulties, for Galloway was an active, muscular man, and Shaw had been a small man, of very poor physique.

Galloway, the Atrorney General concluded, had had the motive, he had had the opportunity—and it also appeared that he had a possible weapon. According to the medical report, the fatal blow had been struck with a heavy, round-headed object, probably a hammer. A hammer with a head of the right size had in fact been found in a locker on Galloway's boat. Admittedly it had been free from blood or other traces of violent use, but it could easily have been cleaned after the attack. No other weapon had been found anywhere, though the banks had been searched and the river dragged. No other suspect had appeared in the case. There was no indication that Shaw had had any other enemies. All the evidence pointed inexorably to Galloway as the murderer.

Wilson's report gave little space to the Crown witnesses. There were very few of them, no doubt because most of the facts on which the prosecution relied were undisputed. The usual formal evidence was given of the finding of Shaw's body and its identification, and of Galloway's arrest. The medical witness conceded in cross-examination that while a hammer could have caused the wound in Shaw's head, it was by no means the only object that could have caused it. Donald Thorpe, who with his girl had reported the quarrel on the boat, said that one of the things they'd heard as they walked past was, "You won't get a penny out of me, you damned blackmailer." It emerged that in view of the violence of the language he'd wanted to stop and listen, and perhaps intervene, but the girl had been scared and had persuaded him to walk on after a moment or two.

Next came the opening for the defense, vigorously presented by a leading Q.C. named Olsen. It was a complete denial that Galloway had either copied Shaw's plot or murdered him. The prosecution's case, Olsen said, was as full of holes as a sieve. Galloway was not a man who needed to steal plots, his whole record showed that. His remarks during the TV interview had been largely jocular and too much shouldn't be read into them. Like other authors, he found himself short of a plot at times, but he'd always managed to produce a good one in the end, and to make a lot of money out of it. His financial embarrassment, though fairly acute, had been purely temporary. Then the jury must consider the practical difficulties in the way of the theft that was alleged against him. They must ask themselves whether Galloway would really have dared to gamble on Shaw first not discovering and, second, not doing anything about, the plagiarism. Would Galloway not have expected that Shaw, an admitted fan of his, would read *Full Fathom Forty* when it was published? Would he not have expected him to be angry? Would he not have realized that Shaw, in the meantime, would probably have submitted his treasured manuscript to some other author for criticism and so be in a position to bring independent evidence of the theft? Again, if Galloway had stolen Shaw's plot, would he not have had the sense to make substantial changes in it instead of taking it over more or less intact? On all grounds, the defense maintained, it was most improbable that Galloway had plagiarized.

What, then, was the explanation of these two almost identical plots? How had it happened? The defense had no doubt about the answer. What had occurred was exactly what Galloway had supposed in the beginning—a rare but not unparalleled example of coincidence. The same newspaper story had inspired both plots and the minds of the two men had thereafter worked along similar lines. It was quite possible that, unknown to either of them, they had at some time read some tale that contained the main elements in both their stories—that, quite unconsciously, they had both drawn on the same source. Very little was known about the subconscious mind, but its great retentive power was universally acknowledged. Seeds sown ten or twenty years before might have germinated now. There had been other instances of the same sort of thing. . . . Here Olsen quoted a number of examples of proved literary coincidence in the past, all of them fairly remarkable. Someone on the defense side had been doing some pretty active research.

As far as the murder itself was concerned, Olsen said, it was most unlikely that Galloway would have gone to the extreme length of silencing Shaw if, as the defense maintained, he knew he was innocent of stealing Shaw's plot. Anger over Shaw's allegations and claims would have been natural, but it was a sense of guilt, not a consciousness of innocence, that drove to deliberate murder in such circumstances. An innocent man would have sought for a safer and less drastic way out of his predicament. It was, in any case, difficult to believe that Galloway would have dared to follow and kill a man so close to his boat, knowing that his association with the man would almost certainly be established and that his motive would come out.

There were many other pointers, Olsen went on, to Galloway's complete innocence of the horrible crime with which he was charged.

Had not the police themselves admitted that he had seemed surprised on hearing of Shaw's death? Was it not true that he had at once volunteered a comprehensive statement covering the whole situation and that he had not departed from it since in any particular? That statement, the defense maintained, had been the work of an impetuous and innocent man, bewildered by events and eager to tell the whole truth as he knew it. The prosecution had suggested that there was something sinister about the finding of a hammer aboard Galloway's boat, but it had already been established that some other weapon might have been used. Besides, on what boat would a hammer not be found? The answer might well be, on the boat of a murderer! If Galloway had used his hammer as a weapon would he not have thrown it away afterward? Its presence on the boat was actually a point in his favor. Was it not true, too, that no trace of blood had been found on Galloway's clothes or on any of his property, and that the evidence against him was entirely circumstantial? It was not part of the defense's task to produce an alternative suspect, but it must be evident to the jury that anyone might have come secretly to the towpath that night and followed Shaw and killed him. The case against Galloway was certainly not proved.

After the defense speech, Galloway had gone into the box. According to Wilson's description of him, he had been nervous and visibly suffering from strain. Olsen had taken him carefully through the whole story again, encouraging him to talk and obviously hoping that the jury would get the impression of a man who had nothing to hide. A salient part of the examination-in-chief dealt with how Galloway had come by his plot. It went like this:

How long have you owned a boat?
I've owned a boat of some kind since I was twenty.
Are you very fond of boats and the sea?
Very.
Are you a practical, competent sailor yourself?
Reasonably competent.

How many books have you had published?

Twenty-two.

How many of them were substantially to do with ships and the sea?

About twelve.

So that in choosing a sea theme for your latest book, you were hardly breaking fresh ground?

By no means.

Had any of your earlier plots been based on real-life incidents that you'd read about in newspapers?

Yes, several.

Sea incidents?

Yes, some of them.

When you said in that television interview that you'd "run dry," what exactly did you mean?

I meant that temporarily I hadn't a plot in mind.

Did you mean that you hadn't any story ideas in your head of any sort?

No, merely that I hadn't a definite idea.

Had that happened before?

Yes, it's a recurring phase with most writers.

Were you worried?

Not in the least.

Why not?

Well, when you've thought up twenty-two plots in your life, you take it for granted you'll be able to think up a twenty-third.

Quite so. Now this plot you actually used—when did the idea for that first enter your mind?

The day I sailed from the Canaries.

Did it come suddenly, as an inspiration?

No, I wouldn't say that.

How did it come?

Well, I knew when I went away that I'd got to to think up a new plot and almost automatically my thoughts turned to ships. At one time I toyed with the idea of trying a new sort of Marie Celeste *mystery, based on the disappearance of a yacht's company in the Pacific, but I couldn't get it right. So I went on thinking and presently I remembered this case of the two liners and the automatic course recorder and I thought I could make something of it. After that, I got down to details.*

Thank you.

The examination covered a lot more ground, but it didn't add much to what was already known. Olsen was still exhibiting his client. He concluded by getting clear denials from Galloway that he had either stolen Shaw's plot or killed him—spoken, Wilson reported, "in a firm voice."

The cross-examination was probing and thorough. The Attorney General also began by taking up the story of how Galloway had obtained his plot:

You say you had this idea for your book at the start of your voyage home?
Yes.
Did you happen to mention it to anyone on board ship?
No.
Did you mention it to anyone at any time?
Not till the book was finished, no.
Therefore there is no independent person who can vouch for the fact that you had this plot in mind at the time you say you did?
No.
When you had this idea on the boat, did you make any notes about it?
No, it hadn't reached that stage.
Did you make any notes when you got to England?
Yes, quite a lot.
And while you were writing the book, did you make any rough drafts or parts of chapters, or type bits which you subsequently discarded?
There was quite a bit of rough work, yes.

Did you keep any of this material—the notes you made, or the rough work?

No, I destroyed it when the book was finished. I always do, to clear the decks for the next one.

So it's true to say that you haven't a single note in your possession, a single sheet of typing, which would help to show how this plot came to you and was developed by you?

I'm afraid not.

That's a pity! Now in this story of yours, there's a good deal of technical information, isn't there, about underwater diving and salvage?

Yes.

Have you ever done any diving or salvage work yourself?

No.

Where did you get your technical information from?

From various sources, over a long period. I've always been interested in the subject and I've read a lot about it. It was pretty familiar ground.

Have you any books at home now, bearing on the subject?

Not specifically on diving and salvage, no.

Can you name any books that you have read on the subject?

Not offhand, no. I did most of my reading a long time ago.

You didn't need to consult any expert about the technical aspects?

No.

So apart from your statement that you had picked up information over the years, there is no actual evidence of the source of your material?

No.

Well, now let us turn to the events of a year last February. Did you at any time mention to anyone that you had received a manuscript and letter from Robert Shaw?

No, it wasn't a matter of any special interest.

If you'd opened it, of course, and decided to make use of it, you naturally wouldn't have talked about it?

I didn't open it.

Why didn't you? Wouldn't it have been natural to show a little curiosity—enough, at least, to page through it?

I was very absorbed in my own story and didn't want to be distracted.

Would it have distracted you to glance at a page to two?

Perhaps not, but I hadn't any desire to. Shaw's letter struck me as very egotistical and I could easily have got involved with him. Once I'd opened the manuscript I'd have had to say something about it. It seemed much better to have nothing to do with it.

If you made up your mind so quickly not to open it, how was it you were so long in returning it?

I had a lot of accumulated correspondence to deal with and I was preoccupied with my own story.

You don't employ a secretary?

Not for my correspondence. I have someone to do my final typing, that's all.

Even without assistance, it wouldn't have taken you long to put a fresh piece of paper round the manuscript and readdress it, would it?

No.

The work of a few moments?

Yes.

But in fact it took you three weeks?

It was three weeks before I posted it, yes, and I've told you why.

Next followed a short passage about Galloway's financial situation.

How did you propose to deal with the heavy income-tax arrears we've heard about if this story of yours had not been a success?

I hoped it would be a success.

Your stories don't always sell for films, do they?

Not always, no.

If this story had not been bought for a film, and at an unusually high figure, would you have been in a position to meet your obligations?

It might have been difficult for me to meet them at once.

Had you any plans for raising money?

I had thought of selling my boat.

You wouldn't have like that?

Naturally not.

Perhaps you would also have had to travel less?

It's possible.

And, in general, to live in a more careful way?

I suppose so.

Finally, the Attorney General turned to the way in which Galloway had handled the problem of Shaw.

When you realized that Shaw suspected you of stealing his story, wouldn't it have been wise to see a solicitor at once?

I think it would. I wish now that I had.

Why didn't you?

Well, to start with, I thought I could handle it myself.

According to your statement, you realized you were in an awkward predicament?

Yes, I did.

Did you, in fact, confide in anyone at all?

No.

You have friends, I take it?

Of course.

But you didn't tell anyone?

No. It was rather an embarrassing situation. I hoped that Shaw might decide to drop the thing.

After your quarrel on the boat, did you still think he might drop it?

No, I didn't think so then.

So did you then write to your solicitor?

I was going to write on the Sunday evening. Monday was a holiday—he wouldn't have been at his office anyway.

When the police came to question you, you still hadn't begun to write to him?

No.

I suggest to you that you never intended to write to him. I suggest that from beginning to end you avoided mentioning your predicament to anyone because you had your own private plans for dealing with it?

If you mean by that that I planned to kill Shaw, it's fantastically untrue.

That will be for the jury to decide.

There was some re-examination. On the question of why Galloway hadn't talked about his plot to anyone, Olsen elicited the fact that he rarely discussed his plots with people unless they were turning out badly and he needed to clarify his ideas, and that this one had gone well from the start. On the matter of the three-week delay in returning Shaw's manuscript, Galloway agreed that he'd considered Shaw's request for a detailed criticism something of an imposition and had therefore not hurried to send the manuscript back. Finally, Olsen asked some further questions on the subject of Galloway's financial tangle and how he'd got into it, and brought out the fact that while he'd been extravagant on occasion to the point of recklessness he'd also been recklessly generous in making gifts to other people, particularly to certain seamen's charities. And that concluded Galloway's evidence.

The final speech for the prosecution was fair but deadly. The Attorney General began by dealing at length with the defense submission that the similarity of the two plots had been a coincidence. It was conceivable, he said, that there could be a considerable measure of coincidence in plot and treatment when two stories were based on the same actual event, but in the view of the prosecution it was inconceivable that there could be such identity in detail as existed in this case. It was, in the accused's own phrase, "against common sense." The jury had had the opportunity to read for themselves both Galloway's book and Shaw's manuscript and on this vital question of coincidence they would have to make up their own minds. He would only draw their attention again to certain specific passages—and here he quoted, at length, four or five passages from each work. He did not believe, he said, that any reasonable person could consider such similarities a matter of coincidence.

The defense, arguing in favor of coincidence, had said that Galloway would never have dared to gamble on getting away with the theft of the plot, but that was very open to question. Men took enormous risks for money. Galloway, a man with a great reputation in his own line, might well have doubted whether Shaw, an unknown amateur, would be able to bring an allegation of plagiarism home to him in any effective way. For one thing, the cost of the litigation involved would almost certainly have been more than Shaw could afford and Galloway would have known that. Considering Galloway's urgent need for a big success, the gamble might well have seemed worth while. It had also been argued that, if Galloway had in fact stolen the plot, he would have made more changes in it. But major changes might well have destroyed its value and minor ones would not have sufficed to prevent Shaw from making his charge of plagiarism. Galloway might well have said to himself, "In for a penny, in for a pound."

Even if coincidence *were* the explanation of the similar plots, which the prosecution did not for a moment accept, the case against Galloway remained. The defense had suggested that if Galloway had not stolen Shaw's plot it was unlikely that he would have killed Shaw, but there was Galloway's own admission, made in his statement to the police, that he had doubted if he would be able to convince other people of his innocence in the matter of the plot. And if he'd thought that he couldn't convince others and that his reputation and livelihood were in jeopardy, he had had a very strong motive for murder. In this connection, the defense had argued that Galloway would never have taken the risk of following and killing a man whom he had such a strong motive for killing, when the motive would probably emerge. But that sort of risk existed in almost every case of murder and it had certainly not prevented determined men from killing in the past. In any case, it was far from certain that the association between Galloway and Shaw would ever have been discovered but for the accident of the quarrel on the boat being overheard. Earlier meetings seemed to have been arranged very discreetly and Galloway might well have thought he was safe.

The jury would have been asking themselves, the Attorney General continued, just how the long and detailed statement which Galloway had volunteered to the police fitted into the prosecution's case. The defense had called it "the work of an impetuous and innocent man." It might equally well have been the work of a clever and guilty one. The substance of it would have emerged in any event, sooner or later, from other sources, or from questioning in court, and there were obvious advantages in getting one's blow in first. Up to a point it had certainly been plausible—but perhaps too plausible. It should not be forgotten that Galloway was a skillful and practiced writer of fiction! As a writer, moreover, he would naturally have been in a position to present his case in a striking and persuasive way. Even so, he had failed to explain, in any convincing manner, how his own story and Shaw's had come to be so very much alike.

Finally, the Attorney General recapitulated the stark facts. Galloway had had the opportunity and the motive. A fierce quarrel had taken place. Shaw had left Galloway's boat, breathing threats. Galloway had known that his reputation, his career, everything, was at stake. The night had been dark, the towpath quiet. A lethal weapon was lying handy. So was the river. Twelve hours later, Shaw had been found dead, murdered. In all the circumstances, could any reasonable man be asked to turn away from Galloway and try to conjure up some alternative murderer, some phantom figure, from the emptiness? The prosecution maintained that the case against Galloway was proved beyond any reasonable doubt.

The defense wound up briefly. Olsen could do little but repeat the arguments he had already used, and make a strong appeal. Stressing again the angle of coincidence, he said, "I implore you, ladies and gentlemen of the jury, not to close your minds to the possibility. Coincidence is a strange thing. How often do you read of a coincidence in real life, in the newspapers, or even perhaps experience one yourselves, and say, 'If that were put in a book, no one would believe it? Can you be certain that this is not such a case? I ask you to consider this question most earnestly."

Finally, the judge. His summing up was heavily against the possibility of coincidence. He, too, read passages from the two stories. He, too, reminded the jury that they must approach the matter as reasonable men, as men of common sense. Was it credible that, by pure chance, such similarities could occur in two works, not once but four or five times? If not, then the inescapable conclusion was that Galloway had stolen Shaw's plot. And just as the prosecution's case would be weakened (though not entirely destroyed) if it could be accepted that the similarities were coincidental and that Galloway had spoken the truth on that matter, so it would be strengthened, and greatly strengthened, if the opposite were accepted.

At the same time, the jury must give due weight to several points raised by the defense which seemed to throw doubt on whether a man like Galloway would have acted as he was accused of acting. In spite of what the prosecution had said, they might think it surprising that Galloway had failed to make greater changes in the story he was supposed to have stolen. They might think that the way he appeared to have underestimated the risk of later trouble with Shaw—if he had stolen the story—had been astonishingly reckless. However, they would bear in mind, too, that if murderers always acted with proper caution and foresight they would probably never get to the point of murder at all. The jury might well decide that so much had been at stake for Galloway as to override ordinary caution. A little homily followed on the subject of circumstantial evidence, which could be as good and conclusive, the judge said, as the evidence of actual witnesses if it ruled out, in the eyes of any reasonable person, all other theories or possibilities—and the summing up ended.

The jury had been out for ninety minutes before returning with their verdict of "Guilty." I wondered why it had taken them so long.

Chapter Five

It was two o'clock before I got to bed, and then I didn't sleep. I lay for hours thinking about the case and the evidence, and about Galloway's incredible folly. I thought how different he must be in his secret heart and mind from Mary's own conception of him. I was too shaken and confused to face up yet to the psychological problems of being in love with a murderer's daughter, but I was growing much more aware of them. My impetuous assurances that nothing had changed now seemed dreadfully facile. Mary was right, of course—everything had changed. For her much more than for me. When I thought of her standing by helplessly through the long, frightening months, watching the shadow creeping up on her father and herself, I no longer felt any surprise that she'd seemed to regard me almost as a stranger. She was a totally different woman, now, from the carefree girl I'd met. Our brief romance must seem a fading irrelevancy. Her harrowing experience, unshared by me, had set her apart. It was out of the question that we could just take up the threads again where we'd dropped them. It might well be impossible to take them up at all. It certainly would be if Mary continued to believe her father innocent, for over this, the most vital thing in her life, there'd be no meeting ground. Yet I desperately wanted to see her again, and I knew that I had to.

I rang her up first thing in the morning and asked if I might come. She said I could and I drove down to Kew about ten. Her manner wasn't quite so distant as it had been when I'd left her the previous night. Then, she hadn't seemed to care very much whether I read up on the case or not, or what I thought about it. Now, as she turned to me in the sitting room, she searched my face as she must have searched the faces of the jury when they'd filed back into the box—hoping against hope. I felt thankful that this time the verdict mattered less.

"Well," she said, "what did you make of it?"

There was no point in pretending. I said, "The evidence is pretty strong, isn't it?"

"It's absolutely overwhelming."

I looked at her in surprise. "You agree about that . . .? Then how is it you can believe he didn't do it?"

"I know him, that's all."

I nodded slowly. There didn't seem to be any useful comment I could make on that.

"I expect you're thinking I'm all heart and no head," she said, "and that I just won't face facts. But surely the way a man is made up is a fact, too?"

"It's not always a demonstrable one," I said.

"It's still a fact to anyone who knows him. And I know that my father *couldn't* have done what they said he did."

"You mean he's incapable of killing anyone?"

"I didn't say that—he's impulsive and fairly quicktempered and I suppose if he was sufficiently provoked, he might lose control of himself and go for someone bald-headed. Anyone might do that. . . . What I'm absolutely sure about is that he'd never creep up behind a man in the dark and hit him with a hammer."

"It's not a very attractive idea, I agree."

"He couldn't do it, I know he couldn't. And I'm equally sure that he'd never steal anyone else's plot."

"Not even if he was desperate for money?" I said.

"He wasn't as desperate as all that. The thing is, he never bothered very much about money—when he had it, he spent it freely, quite often on me or on entertaining his friends or just giving it away—and when he hadn't he earned some more. He worked awfully hard, you know—that picture the prosecution drew of a sort of rich playboy who did a bit of work occasionally couldn't have been more untrue. That's why he wasn't desperate, because he knew he could work hard and get over any temporary jam. Even if he'd had to sell his boat he'd have bought another one later on. . . . Anyway, all that's beside the point. If he'd been on his uppers he wouldn't have stolen anyone else's plot."

"Did you know much about his work?" I said. "Did he talk to you about it?"

"Of course he did. Not when he was actually writing—he'd shut himself up in his flat or on the boat for weeks on end, then, and I'd scarcely see him at all. And he very rarely told me about his plots beforehand because that would have lessened the impact when he showed me the final story. But as soon as the book was typed he'd always bring it straight along to me and he wouldn't be able to rest until I'd read it and discussed it with him and then as often as not he'd go away and make changes. He was terrifically thorough and conscientious. He never supposed he was writing great works of literature, but he really enjoyed turning out a well-carpentered job, the best he could do. He was a craftsman and a very fine one—he took genuine pride in his work. That's why it's so utterly fantastic to think he could have taken over someone else's half-baked ideas. He'd never, never have done it."

She spoke with such certainty and passion that I could scarcely meet her gaze. My own skepticism felt like treachery. I drew on my pipe and began to fill it. After a moment I said, "Well, I'm wide open to conviction, Mary—but what about the evidence?"

"Someone else must have killed Shaw," she said. "It was just a horrible bit of bad luck that Daddy happened to see him and quarrel with him that night."

"What about the two plots . . .? It does seem to me a tremendous amount turns on how those two stories came to be so much alike, because if your father did use Shaw's plot, it strengthens the murder accusation enormously. . . . Do *you* think it was coincidence?"

She was silent.

"Of course," I said, "I haven't read either of the stories yet—that's something I've got to do. But judging by the bits the prosecution quoted, I'd have thought coincidence was pretty well ruled out."

Mary nodded. "I've read both stories, over and over. During the trial I tried to buoy myself up with the coincidence idea, because there didn't seem to be anything else, but I don't think I ever really believed it. And I don't now. *I* think it's out, too."

"Well," I said unhappily, "we've got to be logical. If it wasn't coincidence, and if Shaw didn't copy your father's plot, then your father *must* have copied Shaw's."

"I prefer to be logical the other way round," Mary said. "If it wasn't coincidence, and Daddy didn't copy Shaw's plot, then Shaw *must* have copied Daddy's. Just as Daddy believed in the first place."

"But that's ruled out absolutely by the letter Blundell sent to Shaw," I said. "Unless, of course," I added, "Blundell's letter was a forgery—and I assume the defense looked into that. They certainly seemed to take it at its face value at the trial."

"It wasn't a forgery," Mary said.

"That was gone into, was it?"

"Yes, very thoroughly. The prosecution gave us a photostat copy of the letter, as well as letting us see the original, and Daddy's lawyers got an expert to compare it with some other letters that Blundell had happened to write to Daddy ages ago. It was genuine, all right—the expert hadn't any doubt at all. . . . I've still got the stuff here if you'd like to see it."

"I would," I said.

Mary crossed to a bureau and produced the photostat and the letters and a large magnifying glass that she'd obviously used before. There were two letters from Blundell to Galloway, dated about three years earlier. I glanced quickly through their contents. They seemed to be a private follow-up to some public controversy that both men had taken part in on the subject of state aid for writers. Blundell had been strongly for it, Galloway strongly against it. Galloway had taken the line that if a writer couldn't earn his living by writing, he should do some other job as well and not expect to be wet-nursed. Blundell had taken a poor view of that and in his second letter had accused Galloway, with surprising personal acrimony, of not being interested in what happened to his less fortunate colleagues now that he'd hit the jackpot himself. It wasn't a very edifying correspondence!

I picked up the magnifying glass and, without any expectations, compared the two early letters with the photostat of the one that Blundell had sent to Shaw. I wasn't an expert but I didn't have to be. Worn typewriter letters are almost as individual as fingerprints and it was perfectly obvious that all the correspondence had been typed on the same typewriter. The signatures, too, were the same. Blundell had had a very self-conscious signature with a lot of flourishes, difficult to forge successfully. He'd used a fountain pen in each case, not a ball point, and the pressures of the up-and-down strokes were similar in all the signatures, with none of the breaks or hesitations that usually go with amateur forgery. The signature on the letter to Shaw was a bit more slapdash than the others and sloped away at an angle as though Blundell had penned it in a hurry, but it was unmistakably genuine. I examined the date on the letter to see if it had been altered or tampered with in any way but it hadn't. I asked Mary about the paper Blundell had used for the letter to Shaw, because the photostat didn't show the watermark clearly, and she said it had been a quarto typing paper called Egerton Bond. The paper used in the earlier correspondence was Waterton Bond, but there didn't seem anything significant in the fact that Blundell had changed his paper. He'd probably bought his stationery in small quantities from a local retailer and might easily have got a different sort each time.

I put the magnifying glass down. "Well, that seems conclusive enough," I said. "The letter to Shaw is genuine. Blundell wrote it before your father began his story. Therefore, Shaw didn't copy your father's plot. I don't see how we can get around that."

Mary sat down and lit a cigarette. "I can't accept it," she said.

"But, Mary ..." I began, and broke off. It was useless to try and force logic down her throat. It was horrible that I should seem to be bullying her. If we were ever to establish a new relationship, I'd just have to be patient.

"There must be some explanation," she said.

"What explanation can there be?"

She hesitated. It was as though she had something on her mind that she was reluctant to put into words. Finally she said, "Something to do with Blundell, perhaps."

"How do you mean?"

"Well, I've been thinking about it. . . . I think Blundell must have written his letter to Shaw *after* Daddy's book was published, and pre-dated it."

I stared at her.

"That's how my logic goes, anyhow," she said defiantly. She went through it all again. "Daddy didn't copy Shaw. Therefore Shaw copied Daddy, after Daddy's book was published. Therefore Blundell *couldn't* have seen Shaw's story at the time he's supposed to have written his letter to Shaw. Therefore he wrote it later, and pre-dated it."

I said, "Why would he do that?"

"Perhaps because he hated Daddy. By backing up Shaw's claim that the story was his, he'd be able to ruin Daddy professionally."

I could see now why she'd been reluctant! I said, "You mean you're suggesting it was a frame-up—a conspiracy between Shaw and Blundell?"

"It's not impossible, is it?"

"Shaw did it for the money he hoped to squeeze out of your father, and Blundell from spite?"

"Yes."

"It sounds pretty far-fetched to me."

"It's not as far-fetched as Daddy being a murderer."

"M'm . . . !" Everything came back to that. After a moment I said, "Well, *did* Blundell hate your father? I can see there wasn't any love lost between them, but did he *hate* him?"

"He might have. He always behaved as though he did—that's what I gathered from Daddy, anyway. They used to be on some authors' committee together, and Blundell was always complaining about the amount of time it took up and making nasty cracks about well-heeled writers who didn't have to worry about how they were going to earn a living, and looking meaningly at Daddy. Blundell was one of those writers who have to turn out mountains of books in different names and slog away all the time, and he was very bitter and envious."

"Did you know him?" I asked.

"I met him once, that's all. It was a year last April—the Mystery Writers' Guild was holding an exhibition in London and Daddy was roped in to look after one of the stalls, and I went along to help him during the weekend and Blundell was there. He was a terribly grouchy old man—he wouldn't even speak to Daddy."

I looked at her unhappily. "When did you think all this up—about Blundell and a conspiracy?"

"I've practically just thought of it."

"Because you happened to see that correspondence again?"

"Partly, I suppose ... And the way you put things, there wasn't anything else left."

"I'd say you were clutching at straws, Mary."

"Perhaps—but what else have I got to clutch at?"

"It seems kind of tough on a dead man."

"Not nearly so tough as it's been on Daddy. At least Blundell *is* dead. Daddy isn't."

"Well, I must say it doesn't sound very likely to me. However envious a character Blundell was, I can't see him joining in a thing like that. The motive doesn't seem strong enough. ... You say he was old, too. Would an old man, who hadn't long to live anyway, deliberately set out to destroy a younger one simply because the younger one had been luckier and earned a bit more money? Anyone who went as far as that would have to be absolutely eaten up with hatred—and not just ordinary hatred, but real pathological stuff ... Is there the slightest evidence that Blundell had that sort of feeling about your father?"

"I don't know how much evidence there is," Mary said stubbornly. "There might be quite a lot if we knew more about him."

"What you're doing," I said, "is working backward from your father being innocent, and it's brought you to Blundell, and now you want to find evidence to fit."

"Yes—I admit that."

"And not only to fit Blundell, either. You'd have to be able to prove that Shaw knew about Blundell hating your father—otherwise he'd never have approached him."

"All right—we need to know more about Shaw, too."

She seemed so set on her theory now that I couldn't just brush it aside—wild though I thought it. I must at least appear to give it a little consideration. I sat in silence for a while, letting my mind range freely over the idea of a frame-up and trying to put myself in Shaw's position. It was a pretty bizarre field for speculation, but it was by no means without interest. The obvious starting point seemed to be the package that Shaw had sent to Galloway a year ago last February. On the frame-up assumption, I could see two possibilities about that. The first was that the package had contained some manuscript which Shaw had written and which he'd sent to Galloway for criticism in good faith. He'd then got a dusty answer. He'd felt resentful. He'd noticed that the ribbon round the manuscript hadn't been untied. That had meant that Galloway hadn't even looked at it—that no one had looked at it. The way had thus been wide open for Shaw to copy Galloway's next book and then accuse him of plagiarism. That was one possibility. The other was that Shaw had already had a frame-up idea in his mind before he'd sent the package. That seemed the more likely, because otherwise I doubted if he'd have been so ribbon-conscious. He could have sent the package as a try-on, tying the ribbon in a special way so that he'd know whether it had been undone or not. The manuscript could have been one he'd had by him, or something he'd copied out of an old book. The whole thing would have been a gamble, because if the manuscript had come back opened, he'd have had to abandon any plan he'd had. But it wouldn't have been too big a gamble, because he'd have known that the sort of demanding letter he'd written would probably put Galloway's back up. The chances would have looked pretty good that he'd get the manuscript back unopened. After that he'd have been in a position to go ahead and bring Blundell into the plot.

I outlined my ideas to Mary, and we discussed them for a while.

"Of course," I said, "there's one very practical point we're both overlooking. If it was a frame-up, Shaw would have had to digest your father's book when it came out and rewrite it in his own words and type out a fair copy all in about four weeks, in order to be able to take it to your father on the boat when he did. Could he have done it in the time?"

"I don't see why not," Mary said, "if he was all set for it. Daddy's book was very short—only about forty-five thousand words."

"But Shaw's wasn't, by all accounts."

"No, his was longer, but the work couldn't have been very exacting considering how he wrote. It must be easy to type thousands of words quickly if you're not particular what words you use. And for all we know, Blundell might have given him some help in the week or two before he died."

"H'm ...!" I pondered. "There's not a scrap of real evidence against either of them, is there? Actually, Shaw's behavior struck me as pretty genuine, on the whole. Look at the way he had to go and search out Blundell's letter, for instance, after he told your father about it. There was no question of his coming to the boat prepared to prove his point."

"That could have been a sort of double bluff," Mary said. "He was probably very clever."

"If he worked out a plot like this," I said, "he must have been a near-genius. . . . There's another thing. Did you ever see the original manuscript of Shaw's—the actual one he was supposed to have submitted to your father and Blundell?"

"Yes, I saw it soon after Daddy's arrest, with the lawyers."

"What did it look like? Its condition, I mean."

"Well, it was pretty tatty. . . ."

"Ah! Would it have been if Shaw had just typed it out from your father's book?"

"It might have been. He could have prepared all the sheets beforehand and fingered them until they looked old, and typed on them afterward. We've got to assume he thought of everything. That's why Daddy's in such a mess."

I grunted.

"Anyhow," she said, "there's something you haven't mentioned at all, which I think supports the frame-up idea very strongly. The *title* that Shaw put on the manuscript he sent to Daddy—*The Great Adventure*. Do you realize that that was the one thing Daddy was bound to see even though he didn't undo the ribbon—and that it was so vague it gave no idea of the contents at all? Don't you think that's significant? Obviously Shaw would have to be vague if he intended to make it the title of a story he was going to copy later but didn't know anything about, not even the subject."

That was, I felt, a point—the first real point Mary had made. But it was hardly a decisive one. Lots of titles were vague.

"Well," I said after a moment, "where does all this get us?"

Mary's face, which had become animated during the discussion, clouded again. "I suppose it doesn't get us anywhere very much," she said. "I'd like to find out a lot more things about both Blundell and Shaw, but I wouldn't know how to begin."

"What sort of things?"

"Well, whether they knew each other, in the first place. Whether Shaw knew that Blundell disliked Daddy. Whether they met, and how often. Whether they corresponded with each other. And what they were really like, of course. Particularly Shaw. I'd like to know when he first started writing, and how much he did, and whether he talked about his work. I'd like to know whether he ever mentioned *his* plot to anyone while he was working on it, and where he got *his* technical information about underwater diving from. All about him, in fact."

"That's a pretty tall order," I said. "Particularly as both men are dead."

"I know it is. . . . Of course, it was a pretty tall order for you to track me down, wasn't it?—but you managed it."

I smiled. It looked as though I'd got myself a job! I'd no objection to that—I was ready to have a crack at anything if there was the faintest hope it would produce results. But I didn't want to make any firm promises till I'd thought about it a bit more.

I said, "What *I'd* like to do is read your father's book and Shaw's manuscript. Have you got either or both of them?"

"I've got both." She went to the bureau again and took out a book with a lurid cover showing two men fighting on the bed of the sea, and a wad of typescript. "Shaw's story is just a carbon copy, of course."

I nodded, and put the things in my case. "Well—maybe I'll do a bit of sleuthing," I said. "But it's no good pretending I believe in your Shaw-Blundell frame-up theory, because I don't. Frankly, I think it's moonshine."

"I know," she said. "But then *you* don't believe that Daddy's innocent."

Chapter Six

The office was in a state of August lethargy when I reported for duty after lunch. Ames had already scraped the news barrel for the early staff and could think of nothing better for me to do than page through a stack of magazines for a bright idea. It was a perfect opportunity to catch up on my private reading. I raced through *Full Fathom Forty* in a couple of hours, switched to the manuscript of *The Great Adventure* in the early evening, and by clocking-of time had finished that too.

Both the stories were very much what I'd been led to expect. Galloway's was a brisk, taut job and the excitement was held all the way. He was a professional storyteller who'd completely mastered his medium, and he also had an original turn of phrase now and again that gave his writing distinction. It was the sort of book that anyone would have been proud to write. Shaw's manuscript, on the other hand, was woolly and verbose, with long purple passages of description that scarcely carried the story forward at all and great chunks of unlikely dialogue and never a short sentence where a long one would do. It bore all the marks of the undisciplined amateur who was suffering from a rush of words to the head—but the plot was fine. Stripped of its verbiage, it was exactly the same plot as Galloway's.

By now I was quite sure that coincidence wasn't the explanation of the similarity and that one of the two men had copied the other. True, there were no verbal resemblances, but the order of events, the events themselves, and the behavior and reactions of the main characters were the same. Both men had drawn on the same technical material. The question was, who had been first in the field? During my reading of the two stories I'd kept an eye open for any internal evidence of copying, any phrase or sentiment or attitude that seemed out of character for the writer. But I hadn't been able to find any. Galloway had confident references to a number of places that seemed to suggest first-hand knowledge, and he also had a vivid description of a storm at sea as seen from a small boat which was almost certainly based on experience. Shaw hadn't got those references. Shaw, on the other hand, had made one of his characters go to a record office to check up on some facts and had included some filing detail that only a librarian would have thought of or cared about. Galloway hadn't got that. Whoever had copied whom had done an extraordinarily skillful job of selection and rejection. On the whole I'd have expected Galloway to be the more skillful, though of course I knew much less about Shaw. And perhaps it was a question of cunning rather than of skill.

Back at the flat I put the stories aside and began to think again about Mary's frame-up idea. Without her around to argue its claims, it seemed more unlikely than ever. On its merits I could never have persuaded myself that it was worth following up. But its merits weren't everything. Mary wanted it followed up. That was enough. Because she believed her father innocent and I didn't, there was a tremendous gulf between us. Going to work on her theory would at least provide a temporary bridge. And there was always an outside chance that I might be lucky and discover something useful.

I already knew where Shaw had worked and lived. Now I dug out an old copy of the *Authors' Who's Who* and looked up the entry for Blundell. His address was given as Primrose Cottage, Bear Wood, Little Stamford, Essex. That seemed to be the obvious starting place for him. I turned up Little Stamford in a gazetteer and discovered that it was practically in Suffolk. It would take me a full day to drive out there and make my inquiries. As it happened I had the next day free so I decided to check on Blundell first. I'd have liked to take Mary along with me, but it seemed better not to. Anything we talked about would only be a conscious avoidance of the issue that divided us. And my inquiries would probably go more smoothly on my own.

First thing next morning I got the car out and drove off into Essex. It was a fine, sunny day and there was a good deal of traffic about, but it thinned out as I reached the lanes on the Essex-Suffolk border and I got to my destination well before lunch. Little Stamford turned out to be a delightful, pocket-sized village, with a triangular green, a pond, a few old timbered cottages, and a neat little pub called the Bell. I put my head inside the saloon bar, and there was no one there except the landlord. I went in and ordered a pint of old-and-mild and settled down for a quiet chat, as I'd done for the *Post* in hundreds of similar pubs before. I had no difficulty in getting all the general information I wanted about Blundell. Once I'd bought the landlord a drink and told him I was a reporter and was doing a series of articles about thriller writers, living and dead, I could get by with anything. All landlords know that all reporters are crazy, anyway.

Blundell, it appeared, had been a North Country man of Irish descent who had settled in the south during the thirties. At the time of his death he was a florid, heavily-built, slow-moving man, with a shock of white hair. The landlord guessed that his age had been something between sixty-five and seventy. He'd had a delicate wife whom everyone had liked, but she'd died about five years ago. Since then he'd had a succession of housekeepers, the last being a village woman named Mrs. Pearce. The Bell had been his "local" and it had been his habit to drop in most evenings and drink a glass or two of brandy. He'd been quite a celebrity in the district, but he hadn't been very popular. It seemed he'd turned very cantankerous after his wife's death, which was why his housekeepers hadn't stayed with him—that, and the fact that Primrose Cottage was buried away in a wood nearly a mile from the village. Blundell had liked the solitude, but no one else had. He'd seemed in good health for his age right up to the last day and then he'd suddenly dropped dead of a heart attack. I asked if he'd ever brought any friends to the pub and the landlord said he had, once or twice, when he'd had people staying with him. I described Shaw, but the landlord said he couldn't remember anyone like that. I asked what had happened about the cottage and the landlord said it was up for sale and had been for months. It was a nice little place, he said, but because of its isolated position it wasn't everyone's cup of tea. As Blundell hadn't had any children, it had passed, apparently to a brother in Leeds, a well-to-do manufacturer, who'd taken one look at it when he'd come down for the funeral and put it in the hands of an agent and not bothered about it any more. I asked if Mrs. Pearce was still around and the landlord said yes, she was housekeeping for a colonel at a house called The Oaks. He gave me directions and presently I moved on.

Mrs. Pearce was plump and placid. When I explained who I was and why I was interested she seemed quite ready to talk about Blundell. She'd spent just over a year with him, she said, and though she didn't want to speak ill of the dead it was a fact that he'd been very difficult and crotchety and she didn't think she'd have been able to stick it much longer. Toward the end he'd been drinking heavily, which he couldn't really afford anyway, and it had seemed to make his temper worse and she'd had to warn him she wouldn't stay in the cottage alone with him if he got drunk. Still, she had to admit the drink hadn't prevented him from working hard—he'd been shut up in his room all morning and every morning and sometimes in the afternoons as well if the weather was bad. I asked her about his visitors and she said he hadn't been a very sociable man and there'd only been about three visitors in her time, all of them old like himself. The description of Shaw meant nothing to her, I found, and neither did the name. She felt sure she'd never heard it mentioned, she said—not that Mr. Blundell had talked to her a lot about his affairs. I asked her if Blundell had spent much time away from home and she said he'd traveled up to London quite a bit, just for the day, but not regularly. I said hadn't he ever spent a night away? and she said only when he'd gone to Cornwall once for a holiday. I asked her if she could remember whether he'd been to town much in the few weeks before his death, and she thought a bit and said, no, he hadn't, because at that time he'd been working very hard on a story he'd been trying to get finished—which just went to show, because he'd never managed to finish it and it was still there in the house now. I said was the house still furnished, then, and she said, yes, it was just as Mr. Blundell had left it, because Mr. Blundell's brother hadn't done anything about selling his things.

I thanked her for her help and asked her where the house was. Now that I was here, I decided, I might as well take a look at it. I collected a fresh set of directions, together with the address of the agent's representative in the village who would show me over the place—a Mrs. Whitelaw. In fact, Mrs. Whitelaw wasn't able to come with me as she'd hurt her leg but after we'd had a little chat she said she'd trust me to look round on my own if I'd promise to bring the key back. A few minutes later I was parking the car at the edge of Bear Wood. It was a lovely bit of country, high up and with wide views to the south, but it certainly was lonely. Nothing of the house was visible from the road and if it hadn't been for a "For Sale" board at the entrance to a rutted track I could easily have missed it. I walked along the track for about fifty yards and came upon the cottage in a small clearing among the trees. It was very tiny and rather dilapidated but it had a thatched roof and pink-washed walls and was highly picturesque from a distance. Judging by the footmarks around the place it had been viewed by quite a lot of people, and a broken pane of glass near the handle of one of the lattice windows suggested that someone had taken a look inside without bothering to get the key. Feeling very virtuous I unlocked the door and let myself in.

It wasn't at all a bad cottage inside and I could quite understand why Blundell had liked it. There was a large combined sitting room and dining room downstairs, with a fine fireplace and a lot of old oak. The kitchen was small, but it had been modernized. Blundell must have paid heavily to have the electricity brought from the road, but it was there. The downstairs rooms were rather dark, but the three upstairs rooms were brighter. Two were bedrooms; the third was evidently Blundell's work room. There was a roll-top desk and a filing cabinet; a table with a portable typewriter on it, now shut up in its case; a chair with a worn leather seat, and an array of bookshelves. The room had obviously been tidied up a bit, but otherwise Blundell's stuff was still as he'd left it. There were a couple of old manuscripts on the table, a stick of typing paper, a Roget's *Thesaurus* and a dictionary, some old maps and yellowing newspapers, a folder containing part of a story, and a large copper ashtray.

I didn't very much fancy the idea of poking about among the dead man's effects but by pure chance I'd been given the run of the place and the opportunity seemed too good to miss. If Blundell *had* had any guilty secrets, which I now doubted more than ever, this was the time to look for them. The roll-top desk was locked but I found the key in an unlocked drawer and opened it, releasing the catches of all the other drawers. Then I started to go systematically through the contents. It took quite a while. There was a large file of correspondence, and I glanced at every letter. They were the accumulation of a few months only, the last few months of Blundell's life, and the letter that Shaw must have written submitting his manuscript was not among them. No doubt it had been part of an earlier batch, which had been destroyed. I put the pile back and flipped through some check stubs and had a look at a wad of royalty statements from Blundell's literary agent. They were mostly for small sums and related to books by various authors—all of them, I assumed, Blundell under different pseudonyms. A glance at his bookshelves confirmed that, for they were filled with blocks of books, all thrillers, by the same variety of authors. It looked as though work had been Blundell's life.

I examined the contents of the folder on the table. There were ten chapters of an uncompleted manuscript, evidently the story he'd been trying to finish at the time of his death. It was about a jewel robbery. There were some loose sheets beside it with some notes scribbled on them, also about the jewel robbery. I opened his typewriter and took a sheet of paper from the stack—it was Egerton Bond—and just as a matter of interest I typed out a few words. The typewriter was unmistakably the one that Blundell had used in his correspondence with Galloway and his letter to Shaw. It was an old Royal. Probably he'd had it for years.

I spent over an hour there altogether and I looked at everything. Then I took the key back to Mrs. Whitelaw and set off back to town. By now I had a pretty complete picture of Blundell in my mind. There was only one thing that puzzled me a little and that was that so crotchety a man should have gone to the trouble of reading and criticizing in a friendly way the manuscript of a total stranger. From what I'd heard of him, I'd have expected him to take at least as tough a line as Galloway. But that was the only point of interest. I'd found no indication of any kind that Blundell had met Shaw or known him personally, let alone conspired with him. I'd found no evidence of any special dislike of Galloway. I'd found nothing to suggest that Blundell had ever had anything to do with *The Great Adventure*. On the contrary, all the evidence went to show that he'd been immersed in work of his own right up to the end. My day, I reflected, could scarcely have been more negative in its results. But at least I wasn't surprised.

Chapter Seven

With Blundell virtually out of the picture as a suspect, there seemed less reason than ever to suppose that a check up on Shaw would produce anything helpful. But I knew Mary would want answers to her questions, and I felt a certain curiosity myself about the man who'd become so fatally involved with Galloway. Sharp at nine next morning, therefore, I drove out to the library where Shaw had worked. His successor was shut away in a room of his own, which gave me a chance to talk to the two girl assistants, both of whom had been there in Shaw's time. I told them I was a reporter on the *Post* and that I was collecting material for a complete history of the Shaw case and wanted to find out everything about Shaw that I could. They were quite amenable and chattered away freely in the intervals between stamping books. Very soon I had as good a picture of Shaw as I'd had of Blundell.

He had been, it appeared, a quiet, mild-mannered little man—a bit humorless, but entirely inoffensive. He'd been unmarried and had lived with his sister, a Mrs. Green. He'd dressed neatly, spoken correctly, and always behaved impeccably. He'd been considerate to his staff, and though no one had been exactly fond of him, no one had disliked him. He'd been very conscientious about his job, always arriving on time and putting in a good day and never leaving early. Off duty, I learned, his great interest and hobby had been crime and mystery books. He'd been a real addict—not just as a reader but as a student of the *genre*. He'd contributed articles on the subject to the *Librarian* and various book trade papers, attended lectures by thriller writers whenever he could and taken part in the discussions, and built up a big collection of thrillers at home, going back years. Both the girls had known that he'd been trying to write a crime story himself about eighteen months ago—it seemed he'd often stayed in and worked on it during his lunch hour. I asked them if he'd told them what the plot was about, but they said no. I also asked if they could remember whether he'd ever shown any special interest in a writer named Blundell, but they didn't think he had.

From the library I drove on to the house in Croydon which Shaw had shared with his sister. It was more than four months since Shaw had died and I thought Mrs. Green should have got over the worst of her distress by now. Number 12a Cavendish Road turned out to be a modest, semi-detached villa in a respectable road where every house had its small neat garden and its small neat garage and its television antenna. Mrs. Green answered the door herself. She was a thin, anemically pretty woman of about thirty with wispy hair and a discontented mouth and a genteel-cockney voice. Her face brightened when she saw me, but only for a moment—it appeared she'd just advertised a furnished room to let and had thought I might be an applicant. I apologized for not being and told her who I was and why I'd called. I said I was sorry to be harking back to an old tragedy but there was still a lot of public interest in the Shaw case and I was most anxious to get all the information I could. She looked most unforthcoming and I felt sure she was going to turn me down. I added that of course I'd be quite prepared to pay for any information. At the mention of money her interest quickened perceptibly and she asked me what I wanted to know. I said perhaps I could take a look at her brother's room first, because I was interested to see where he'd done his writing. She said I could look if I liked but there wasn't much to see because that was the room she was letting and she'd just cleared it out and redecorated it. I said I might still be able to get an impression and she led the way upstairs and into the front room. It had been cheaply furnished as a bed-sitter, and there was a strong smell of distemper from the bright pink walls.

"His desk was over there by the window," she said, "and his bookshelves used to stand against the wall there. His papers and things are in the back room—what's left of them. Would you like to see them?"

I said I would and she took me across the landing and showed me four large wooden boxes. Three of them contained books and various odd-looking bits of junk and the other was full of folders and files and what looked like personal papers. Here, evidently, was an appreciable slice of Robert Shaw's life. I'd have liked to examine the stuff, but there was far too much to go through there and then.

I said, "I suppose these things belong to you, now, Mrs. Green?"

"Oh, yes," she said, "Robert left everything to me. Not that he had much, really."

"What are you going to do with them?"

"Well, I've been meaning to send the books to a secondhand shop in Croydon—the man said he might give me a pound for them. The other boxes are mostly rubbish. Robert kept an awful lot of rubbish—he just couldn't bring himself to throw papers away. This is nothing to what there was—I burned a lot in the garden."

I said, "Would you take five pounds for what's here?"

She looked at me in astonishment. "Five pounds!" she said. "It's not worth that!"

"It might be to me—and, anyway, that would include whatever information you could give me about your brother. I'd be very glad to pay it. I can give you a check when I leave and take the things with me. What do you say?"

Her thin shoulders rose in a shrug. "Well, if you really mean it, I won't say no. I could certainly do with the money."

I said most people could these days and asked her if she had any family and she said she had—two boys, aged seven and five, who were at school. By now I was over the hump with her—once she'd started talking about her own affairs she went on. Her husband, it appeared, had left her three years ago. He paid her the maintenance the court had ordered and that was all, and it didn't go far. Things hadn't been so bad while Robert had been living with her but now it was very hard. She did a bit of sewing work in Croydon three

72

mornings a week, but she had to look after the house and the children so she couldn't do a proper job. She'd sold everything of Robert's that had been worth anything, like his clothes and his typewriter, and she'd got enough for his old car to buy new furniture for the room she was letting, and now it was a case of trying to make ends meet whatever way she could. I had a feeling she was missing her late brother a lot, but that it was financial care she was overcome with rather than grief.

Directly I could get a word in, I steered the conversation back to Shaw's activities. I said I gathered he'd always wanted to be a writer and she said, yes, only he hadn't had much luck, and the book he'd written hadn't brought him much luck, had it? I agreed that it hadn't and asked her when he'd first started writing and she said he'd been sending articles to newspapers ever since she could remember, but he'd only tried stories in the last year or two. I asked her if he'd spent much time writing and she said almost all his spare time while he'd been living with her—his typewriter had been a perfect nuisance, rattling away like a machine gun and preventing the children from going to sleep. I said I supposed he'd been a pretty expert typist and she said not really, he'd only used two fingers, but he'd done so much of it that he'd got quite fast. I asked her if he'd discussed his writing with her and she said hardly ever. I said what about the book that had given all the trouble, surely he'd told her about his wonderful plot, and she said, no, he hadn't said a word about it till last March when he'd discovered that John Galloway had stolen his idea. I asked her if he'd ever mentioned Galloway to her before then and she said, yes, a long while back, after his story had been returned without even a friendly word. He'd been very fed up about that. She thought Galloway must be an absolute monster and it was a wicked thing he hadn't been hanged as he deserved. Some friends of hers had said she ought to sue him for damages the way Robert had intended to and she'd thought of asking a lawyer about it, only she had enough worries to be going on with. I nodded sympathetically and asked her if Robert had said anything to her about sending his story to the other man, Blundell, and she said not at the time, she hadn't heard about that until just before Robert's death. She said Robert had usually told her only about things that had annoyed him and of course he must have been pleased to hear from Blundell. As far as Shaw's relations with Blundell were concerned, she couldn't help me at all. Robert had only mentioned him that once, she said, so she couldn't say whether they'd known each other well or not, or whether they'd continued to correspond after Robert had got his story back. They might have, because Robert had always enjoyed writing to authors about their books and about crime. Personally she'd never thought much of Robert's interest in crime, she thought it was morbid, particularly the things he'd collected. I asked her what things and she said, well, for one thing there was a sort of cotton bag that had been put over the head of some murderer on the gallows—it was in one of the boxes I was taking away and I was welcome to it! I had the impression again that Mrs. Green hadn't really liked her brother very much.

By now I'd exhausted my questions. I wrote out a check and told her if she came across anything else of Robert's I'd be glad to have it. Then she helped me carry the four boxes downstairs and a passing milkman gave me a hand getting them onto the roof of the car, and I drove to the office for lunch and my two o'clock stint.

Chapter Eight

I telephoned Mary that evening and gave her a full account of my busman's holiday. I said that as far as I'd been able to discover both Blundell and Shaw had been absolutely genuine and there was nothing at all to suggest they'd ever met each other. I said I hadn't quite finished the inquiry into Shaw as I'd got hold of some of his belongings and hadn't had time to look at them yet. She said she'd like to go through them with me and we arranged that she should come over to my flat first thing in the morning.

She arrived well before ten. She was obviously far from happy about my findings, but her manner toward me was much more forthcoming and friendly than it had been. She said it was nice of me to have gone to so much trouble when I hadn't expected any results, anyway, and I felt glad I'd made the effort.

We got down straight away to investigating Shaw's belongings. I turned the three boxes of books out on the floor in a dusty heap, and we dipped here and there but found nothing to linger over. The bulk of them were thrillers, many of them paperbacks. It was an impressive collection if you happened to be interested in the progress of the thriller through the ages, for it included practically all the famous classics of detection from Wilkie Collins and Edgar Allan Poe onward, as well as books by many writers I'd never heard of. But it didn't tell us anything about Shaw that we hadn't known already, and we soon pushed them aside and turned to the other box.

First came a lot of museum junk. There was the executioner's bag that Mrs. Green had mentioned and a length of hemp rope with a label on it saying it was part of a hangman's rope that had been used in an actual execution, which Mary didn't find very amusing. There were several other objects of criminal interest but they were less macabre—a plaster cast of a footprint with another label on it, a woolen thread that had led to the capture of some murderer, a bag of counterfeit coins, a pair of knuckle dusters and a jemmy, and various other relics. Underneath were some more books, mostly reference works—one about fingerprints, one about poisons, one of forensic medicine, and several in the "Great Trials" series. There was also a book on *How to Become a Writer*. There were two folders of typed short stories by Shaw—all of them, at a casual glance, as wordy as *The Great Adventure* had been. There was a thick wad of rejection slips from newspapers and magazines. There was also a file of correspondence, which we went through carefully. It was incomplete, and didn't tell us much beyond confirming what we already knew, that Shaw off-duty had had a single-track mind. There were several letters from editors of book trade periodicals, mostly about some aspect of the thriller business. There was a letter from the secretary of the Mystery Writers' Guild regretting that Shaw couldn't be accepted as a member until he'd had a crime story actually published. There was a letter from a crime writer named Flowers admitting that trains to Tilbury ran from Fenchurch Street and not from St. Pancras, as he'd said in his last book, and thanking Shaw for pointing it out. There was nothing at all from Blundell.

We continued to delve. There was a typed document entitled *A Study of the Plots of 200 Detective Stories*, by Robert Shaw, a sort of monograph on which much labor had evidently been spent. There were some publishers' lists and some more correspondence. About the last thing we picked out was a program of the Mystery Writers' Guild exhibition that had been held in April of the previous year.

"That's the exhibition I went to," Mary said, riffling through its pages. "It looks as though Shaw went, too."

"He would!" I said. "It probably made his year for him."

"If he did," Mary said, suddenly very alert, "it means that he had at least one opportunity to meet Blundell and talk to him, because Blundell was there."

I gave an inward sigh—she was still clutching at straws. "It wouldn't have been much of an opportunity," I said. "If I know those exhibitions, there was a milling crowd and a frightful din going on and no chance to do any serious talking at all."

"There was a big crowd, yes—scores of thriller writers, and the place was seething with fans. But once Shaw had made his contact he could have taken Blundell aside."

"I just can't see it," I said. "The first approach would have had to be made with tremendous care. Blundell would have had to be probed slowly and cautiously. I can't believe it could have been done there and then. And, as I told you, there's not a shred of evidence that they ever met again. None at Blundell's end, and none at Shaw's."

"If they were planning a crime together," Mary said, "they'd naturally have kept their meetings secret."

"In the later stages, perhaps, but not at first—not while Shaw was doing his probing and the acquaintance was ripening. And there'd have had to be a great many of those meetings—you'd need to know a hell of a lot about a man and how he was likely to react before you could breathe even a hint of a joint criminal enterprise to him. It would have been a long, arduous job, particularly with an old man like Blundell, who was pretty much of a stay-at-home anyway. It's just not credible that a close relationship could have been built up without anyone knowing about it. ... Honestly, Mary, if I thought there was one chance in a thousand of getting anywhere with this idea of yours I'd be all for it, but I'm convinced it's an absolute blind alley. I don't believe for a moment that Shaw and Blundell conspired together. I think the whole thing's quite fantastic."

I'd spoken more emphatically than I'd intended, but Mary had to be prized away somehow from the preposterous theory she was still clinging to. She turned very pale.

"If you're right," she said slowly, "there's no explanation of Blundell's letter to Shaw except that Daddy's guilty."

I didn't reply to that. There wasn't any need.

She sat very still, holding the exhibition program listlessly between her fingers. I wondered if this was the moment to urge her to snap out of things and face up to the truth, but I decided it wasn't. She looked too hard hit. I began to put the scattered papers back into the box. The gulf was between us again, deeper than ever.

I'd almost finished when she suddenly gave an exclamation. I turned quickly. She was staring at the back of the program. She no longer looked listless. I said, "Found something interesting?" She didn't answer at first. She just sat there, frowning. After a moment she got up.

"Peter, have you a sheet of typing paper?"

"Why, sure . . .!" I went and fetched her a piece. She folded it across the middle and took a fountain pen from her bag.

"I wonder if I might have your autograph?" she said.

She'd placed the folded sheet on a thin book and was holding it out to me, her thumb keeping the paper in position. I took the pen and scribbled my name on the paper. She opened it out and studied it for a moment. Then she picked up the exhibition program.

"It says here, 'Visitors to the Exhibition are cordially invited to seek the autographs of their favorite crime writers.' Suppose Shaw collected Blundell's! Look at this!"

She showed me the paper I'd signed. The way she'd held it I'd signed it about two-thirds of the way down the sheet, at a slightly odd angle. I remembered that Blundell's signature in the photostat had been at a rather unusual angle too.

"If I were to type a letter above your signature now," Mary said, "I'm sure I could make it seem like a genuine letter from you."

I looked at her doubtfully. "It's a pretty corny idea, Mary."

"It may be, but it's exactly the sort of idea a man like Shaw might have had. He could have got it from one of his two hundred thriller plots."

I thought about it for a bit. I could see points in its favor. I remembered how out-of-character it had seemed to me that a bad-tempered man like Blundell should write such an amiable letter to an importunate stranger. If Shaw had faked the letter after all, that was explained. . . . But there were insuperable objections.

"Let me get this clear," I said. "Is it your notion that Shaw just happened to collect Blundell's autograph because he was a fan and that when Blundell died he remembered he'd got it and that gave him his idea for a frame-up plan so he went ahead and copied your father's story?"

"Something like that."

"Well, I don't think it's possible. Shaw might just about have had time to copy your father's book in the four weeks between its publication and the day he took his manuscript to the boat. But if he hadn't started copying till after Blundell died, that would have cut his time to a mere couple of weeks or so and if he'd typed like a madman every night he couldn't have done it—not with the rewriting, to. I'd say it was out of the question."

"All right," Mary said, changing her ground rapidly, "perhaps he didn't just *happen* to collect the autograph. Perhaps he'd already got the frame-up idea in mind and collected it deliberately, knowing he was going to copy Daddy's book when it came out and that he'd need a supporting letter."

I shook my head. "The autograph wouldn't have been any use if Blundell hadn't died, because he could have repudiated the letter. And Shaw couldn't possibly have counted on his death."

"He might have hoped for it. . . . You said Blundell was a heavily built man who drank a lot of brandy."

"Shaw would hardly have known about that," I said. "Anyway, brandy's not exactly cyanide—Blundell might easily have lived for another five years."

"M'm . . .! I suppose he did die naturally?"

"His doctor must have been satisfied. Heavens, you're not suggesting that Shaw bumped him off, are you?"

"I just wondered. . . ." She was looking again at the exhibition program. After a moment, she said, "It says here, 'Up to eighty well-known crime writers will be in attendance during each day of the Exhibition.'"

"Well?"

"Couldn't he have got an autograph from each of them?"

"How would that have helped?" I said. "He still wouldn't have known that one of them would die."

"I should think he might have reckoned on one out of eight dying before Daddy's book came out. A lot of them were pretty ancient."

"Suppose one hadn't?" I said.

"Well, he could have hung on for a bit, couldn't he?—someone would have been bound to die in the end. He could have produced his letter later on and said he'd only just read Daddy's book. I don't mean years later, but months, anyway."

"H'm . . . Well, it's not *absolutely* impossible, I suppose. . . . I'm just trying to imagine him, though, rushing about at that exhibition collecting eighty autographs as a speculation."

"Perhaps he didn't collect eighty—perhaps he just concentrated on the elderlies. That would have been much quicker."

"True . . . Okay, let's agree for the sake of argument that that takes care of the signature. We're still left with the text—what about that? Blundell's letter to Shaw was definitely typed on Blundell's typewriter."

"Then Shaw must have had access to it," Mary said.

"When?"

"After Blundell's death, I should think. It doesn't seem to have been very difficult. After all, you typed a few lines on it yourself."

"Yes, but then I wasn't planning a crime. I can't see Shaw calmly going along and asking for the key of Blundell's cottage when he was plotting to . . ." I broke off. "Just a *minute*, though!"

"What, Peter?"

"The window! There was a broken pane of glass in one of the downstairs windows, right next to the handle."

"There you are, then—he broke in! It would have been safe enough as long as he was careful—you said yourself the cottage was buried in the trees. And he had a car, hadn't he?—he could have driven there one evening after work. Probably soon after the funeral, before Blundell's things could have been moved."

"How would he have known the place was empty?"

"He wouldn't for sure, I suppose, not until he got there, but houses quite often are left empty for a while after a funeral, because people tend to go away. He'd have had to do a bit of reconnoitering, of course, but once he'd found there was no one about the rest would have been easy. He could have dashed off that letter in five minutes."

I pondered. It was physically possible—but I could see a lot more objections. I said, "He'd have been taking a good deal for granted in all this, wouldn't he, besides a convenient death?"

"How do you mean?"

"Well, relying on being able to complete his faked letter by typing in the text, for one thing. The author who died might have been one of those who do all their writing by hand. Then Shaw's autographed sheet of paper would have been useless."

"There can't be many authors who don't use a typewriter these days," Mary said.

"Enough to make an extra hazard, I should think. Especially among the older hands."

"Well, perhaps he checked up in some way. He could have written letters to all his prospects—then he'd have known whether they typed or not, from the answers he got."

"That would have been a job."

"If it was to help his plot along," Mary said, "he'd probably have got quite a kick out of it. Or perhaps he found some simpler way—perhaps he just *asked* them all at the exhibition. ..." She suddenly broke off, her eyes large and bright. "Wait—I think I've got it ... !"

I waited.

"There was a special stand at the exhibition showing samples of work by various authors. It was one of the attractions for the fans. Each author had sent in a typical page of corrected manuscript and the pages were all pinned up on a board. Shaw would only have had to look at that and he'd have known straight away which authors used typewriters and whose autographs to go for."

I nodded. She'd covered the point and covered it well. But already

I could see a worse snag ahead. "There's still the question of paper," I said.

"What about paper?"

"The letter from Blundell to Shaw was on Egerton Bond, wasn't it? The paper I found on Blundell's desk in the cottage was Egerton Bond, too. That's fine if Blundell wrote the letter himself—it ties up nicely. He just used a lot of Egerton Bond. But if Shaw faked the letter, on paper he'd chosen himself a year and a half earlier, then it's a pretty odd coincidence, don't you think?"

"It could be just that—a coincidence."

"Well, I don't know. There must be scores of different kinds of typing paper and Shaw could have picked any one of them. He could have picked, for instance, Waterton Bond, which was what Blundell was using when he wrote to your father a year or two back. But no, he picked Egerton Bond, the sort Blundell happened to have been using lately. I'd say it was a strong point against you, Mary."

"There may be some quite good explanation," she said.

"Perhaps Shaw noticed that Blundell's exhibit on the board was Egerton Bond?"

"That can't be it. Blundell was only one of his prospects, don't forget. You're not suggesting that Shaw made a note of the paper every author had used and then slipped out and bought some of each kind and presented the right sort for each autograph? There are limits!"

She was silent for so long that I thought she really had no answer this time. But I was wrong. Suddenly she cried, "*I* know ...!"

"Well?"

"Perhaps Blundell never used Egerton Bond at all! What was there to prevent Shaw taking a ream or two of Egerton Bond with him to Blundell's cottage and exchanging it for whatever was there—because it was the sort he'd used for his letter? He could have planned to do that from the beginning, whoever it was who died. ..."

"H'm!—very ingenious!" I said.

"Well, he could, couldn't he?"

"I don't see why not. ... All right, let's say that clears up the paper question. I can still see another objection, though—looking at the thing from Shaw's point of view. When he came to write his letter on the paper that Blundell had autographed—after Blundell's death—he had to put a date on it, didn't he?"

"Of course."

"Well, how would he have known what Blundell might have been up to on the date he chose? Suppose it had been discovered afterward—suppose *we'd* discovered, for instance—that Blundell had been seriously ill around that time, and not writing letters, or that he'd been in America, or something? Wouldn't that risk have worried Shaw?"

"No," Mary said, "because the date on the letter was April 12, and that was the day before the exhibition opened. Shaw would have known that Blundell was around then. And *I'd* say that's rather significant."

I nodded again, and fell silent. I had no more objections. I didn't feel as excited as Mary obviously did—I hadn't her faith—but I was deeply interested and certainly more hopeful than I'd been at any time before. This new case against Shaw, hypothetical though it was, seemed to me to be on a completely different plane from the conspiracy-with-Blundell idea. The air of fantasy had gone. I no longer had to struggle with an utterly unconvincing motive like the one that Mary had tried to attribute to Blundell. If Shaw had planned a frame-up on his own he'd done it from the most convincing of all motives—for the hard cash he hoped to get out of it. Given a sufficient degree of cunning, the thing was feasible—and Shaw somehow seemed to fit the part. A man who'd taken such exceptional pleasure in dissecting other people's fictional plots might well have thought himself capable of planning a real one of his own. I could just imagine him sitting up in that room of his evening after evening, quietly spinning his web and reveling in his own ingenuity. He was exactly the right type for it—the mild, inoffensive, retiring type! What was more, there were aspects of his behavior that I hadn't attached much importance to when I'd been thinking in terms of the unlikely Shaw-Blundell theory, but which now fitted in well.

The fact that he hadn't mentioned the subject of his plot to anyone, for instance. The fact that he'd told his sister about sending his manuscript to Galloway but not said a word to her about sending it to Blundell. Of course, nothing was certain. We hadn't in any sense established that Shaw *had* faked the crucial letter from Blundell—we'd merely gone some way to establishing that he *might* have, which was quite a different matter. What we wanted now was positive evidence.

As I thought back to the all-important letter, I found myself wondering if the defense experts had gone into the question of the typing "touch" in the various exhibits they'd been shown—the letter to Shaw, and the Blundell letters to Galloway. Would Blundell and Shaw have had a different "touch"? Probably they'd both been two-finger typists—most men were. Would that, I wondered, have emphasized differences, or concealed them? I was a two-finger man myself—perhaps I could judge from my own work. I felt in my pocket again for the bit of typing I'd done on Blundell's typewriter and scrutinized the letters—but I couldn't detect any distinctive pattern of pressures. . . . What I did see, though, suddenly gave me a startling new idea.

I looked across at Mary, deep in her own thoughts—and hesitated. It was a bright idea—but it might turn out to be a disastrous one.

"What is it?" she said.

"I've just thought of a way we could test Shaw's letter. The thing is, I don't think it could prove that the letter was a fake. It *could* prove that it wasn't a fake!"

"Oh . . .! Well, go on."

"You know how a typewriter gets clogged up after a while if you don't clean it—the letters, I mean—and it shows in the typing?"

She nodded.

"I've just been looking again at the bit of typing I did on Blundell's machine. The letters are quite badly clogged—especially the *e* and the *a*." I showed her.

"Well?"

"Well—if Shaw did fake his note on Blundell's typewriter after Blundell's death, the state of the letters would have been about the same as when I used it, because no one else would have touched it in between."

"And the photostat would show if they were," Mary said.

"Yes—but this is the point. If the letters in the photostat *are* clogged, it means the question of who typed the letter is still open. Shaw could have done it, or the typewriter could have been in the same sort of state eighteen months ago and Blundell could have done it. But if they're *not* clogged, it means that Shaw didn't do the typing. It could be the end of our new theory—the end of everything."

"Let's go and see," Mary said.

We drove straight over to Kew. It was a horribly tense and silent journey. I almost wished I hadn't had the damned idea, but it was too late now. The moment we reached the flat, Mary rushed to the bureau and got the photostat. Together we bent over it.

The letters *a* and *e* were clogged!

"Good for you!" I said softly.

"You see, Peter! It fits—it *all* fits. Oh, Peter, I really do believe we're onto something at last. Darling!"

She threw her arms round my neck and hugged me. It wasn't a romantic embrace, but it was something. It looked as though the ice was really breaking up at last.

Chapter Nine

I drove to the office that afternoon in a much more cheerful frame of mind. Mary's enthusiasm had been infectious. The mere possibility that Galloway might after all have been the innocent victim of a plot and that everything might yet come right was enormously stimulating. But the attempt to change Mary's new idea from an outside chance to a certainty was going to be a lot tougher than theorizing, and I hadn't a clue where to begin. The fact that the trail was stone cold made things infinitely more difficult. There wasn't a hope that anyone would remember whether one insignificant little man had in fact collected a sheaf of autographs at an exhibition held eighteen months ago. There wasn't a hope, at this stage, of checking whether Shaw had actually bought a ream or two of Egerton Bond paper at any time. There was equally little prospect that I'd be able to get any confirmation of a journey made into Essex so long ago, unless Shaw had been much more careless about it than his otherwise close attention to detail suggested. Back in the spring, I might have been able to find his footprints at the cottage—but not now.

I wondered if there was any chance that experts might be able to draw more helpful conclusions than I'd done from the clogged letters in the photostat and in my bit of typing. I'd had a good look at both exhibits through Mary's magnifying glass, but all I'd been able to see was that the letters looked similar. Perhaps, I thought, a microscopic examination might *prove* that Blundell's letter to Shaw had been typed on Blundell's typewriter since Blundell's death. I wasn't very sanguine, but it seemed worth looking into—and if I was going to look into it, it ought to be done quickly, while Blundell's typewriter was still available as evidence if necessary. I decided that I'd talk to Forbes, our crime man, that evening and see if he could put me in touch unofficially with one of the Yard's experts.

I got to the office just before two. The place was very quiet and the Reporters' Room was empty. I went into the News Room to see what Jones, the Deputy News Editor, had for me, and he handed me a snippet from an evening paper about a man named Crawford who lived at Acton and had had the good fortune to buy a sheet of unperforated stamps at a post office. Would I go and interview him, Jones said. It wasn't much of a job, but at least it would get me out of the office. I stood chatting for a moment or two, and then a boy brought me a parcel that had come for me that morning and I returned to the Reporters' Room to see what was in it. I didn't know the handwriting, but the postmark was Croydon. I opened it, and it was from Mrs. Green. There was a note inside saying she was sending me a few more things of her brother's that she'd overlooked—he'd left them at the library and the library had sent them on to her some months ago and she'd put them in a cupboard and forgotten about them. She hoped they'd be useful to me. I hoped so, too. This was a moment when I badly needed a fresh lead, and the smallest thing might be enough to set me off on some promising track. I tore off the inner covering and spread out the contents. There were a few books and papers, some newspaper cuttings, and some sheets of typed manuscript. I picked up one of the books and glanced at the title. It gave me a sudden, highly unpleasant jolt. The title was *A Manual of Underwater Diving*, and it had Shaw's name and a date nearly two years old on the fly leaf.

That was only the beginning. With mounting consternation I examined the other things. There were three books about underwater diving, each with Shaw's name inside. All of them had passages marked and underlined, with marginal comments and cross references, as though they'd been much used and studied. There were four newspaper cuttings on the same subject, clipped from papers published nearly two years before. There was a notebook, half filled with notes relating to the plot of *The Great Adventure*, including ideas for character names—some of which I remembered as having been used in Shaw's story—and chapter headings, and jottings about plot development. There was also a typed chapter of the story, with some penciled alterations. It was slightly different from the version I'd read in the finished manuscript and was evidently a draft. Unless all this stuff was part of some very elaborate deception, the conclusion was inescapable. Shaw had indeed built up the disputed plot from his own sources, as he'd said, and long before Galloway had ever thought of it.

There was worse to come. At the bottom of the pile I found a letter from another thriller writer, commenting on Shaw's story. This time it was from a man named Richard Dancy, an author whose name was moderately well known to me. It was from an address in Elford Square, off Baker Street, and it said:

Dear Mr. Shaw,

Many thanks for your kind remarks about my books and for letting me see your own manuscript. I've now read it and I'm returning it to you under separate cover. I think the plot is jolly good, but since you ask me to be quite frank I'm bound to add that in my view the story lacks the professional touch and badly needs an expert overhaul if it's to have any chance of finding a publisher.

> With all good wishes,
> Yours sincerely,
> Richard Dancy

The letter was dated March 10 of the previous year, a month earlier than Blundell's.

I put it down on the desk, feeling pretty sick. It was only too clear now that all the stuff Mary and I had thought up about Shaw had been sheer wishful thinking. My earlier skepticism had been right. Blundell's letter was genuine—that was confirmed now. Galloway *had* copied Shaw's plot. I'd been a fool ever to doubt it. I ought to have remembered that Shaw had told Galloway he'd shown his story to other people as well. I ought to have realized that fresh evidence might turn up. I ought to have been more wary. As it was, my intervention had been a disaster. First I'd gone along with Mary, tacitly accepting her theory; then I'd produced the facts that had destroyed it. Now I had the prospect of breaking the bitter news to her. What had happened was disappointing enough for me—it would be sheer tragedy for her. Yet I'd got to tell her. If I didn't, she'd expect me to go on making inquiries on the basis of her theory. In any case, it was no good trying to keep the truth from her—she would have to face it. And this time there'd be no way out; even Mary couldn't explain *this* letter away. It was conclusive.

. . . Or *was* it? I picked up the letter again and had another look at it. Actually, it wasn't conclusive as it stood, for I saw now that it didn't mention Shaw's manuscript by name or refer to any specific point that would have identified it. The manuscript *could* have been some other one that Shaw had submitted to him. I didn't believe it for a moment, in view of the other contents of the parcel, but Mary would probably raise the point. I'd better check it. I could call in at Dancy's on my way to Acton and if he was home I could settle it once and for all.

I picked up the car outside the office and twenty minutes later I was turning into Elford Square. It was a place of gracious Georgian houses, three stories high and terraced and mostly divided into flats. Dancy lived at number 8. I parked behind a dilapidated station wagon with a lot of country mud on it and climbed the steps. Dancy's was the top flat. I rang the bell and waited and in a few seconds Dancy himself came down. He was a pink, plump, jolly-looking man, with a pink bald head as smooth as an egg, and blue eyes. I guessed he was about forty-five, though his baldness made him look older. I told him my name and that I was a reporter on the *Post* and asked him if he could spare me a moment or two.

"Well, you've caught me at a bad moment," he said. "I'm just going to drive my fiancée down to Eastbourne. Still, if you don't mind making it snappy. . . . Come on up."

I followed him to the top floor. At the entrance to his flat three black Scotties made a simultaneous rush at me, barking gruffly, and I heard a woman's voice inside calling them to heel. "Don't take any notice of them," Dancy said. "Oh, darling, this is Mr. Rennie from the *Post*. . . . My fiancée, Lavinia Hewitt."

I said "How d'you do?" to Miss Hewitt. She was a tall, thin, angular woman of about thirty-five, with a face of almost incredible plainness. The clothes she was wearing—a dun-colored cardigan, a shapeless tweed skirt, and heavy, flat-heeled shoes—did nothing to improve the effect. I decided she must be very intelligent or very goodhearted. She was still trying to call off the Scotties, not very effectually. She said "I *do* hope you like dogs, Mr. Rennie," in a rather gushing voice. I said I did. She said she could tell I did or they wouldn't like me so much. Before I could get even a word with Dancy, she was telling me that she had twenty-three dogs at her boarding establishment near Lewes, as well as nine cats, five budgerigars and a tortoise, and if ever I wanted any interesting little bits about animals for my paper she'd be delighted to give them to me. I thanked her, and at last Dancy managed to shepherd me into his study. "We shan't be more than a few minutes, darling," he said, and shut the door on the dogs with a look of relief. "Well, now, what is it, Mr. Rennie?"

I told him, briefly. I said I was planning to write up the Shaw murder case in my private capacity and that I'd come across a letter from him among Robert Shaw's effects and that was why I'd called. I showed him the letter.

"That's right," he said, after a moment. "Shaw sent me his manuscript to read. Bit of a nerve, of course, making demands like that on a complete stranger, but I thought I might as well have a look at it—I like to treat young writers civilly when I can. Not that I did *him* much good, poor devil."

"What was the manuscript about?" I said—and waited for the knife to fall.

"Why—it was the story there was such a fuss about at John Galloway's trial. The two liners and the diving—the plot that Galloway said was his."

So there it was!

"Well—thank you," I said. "That's really all I wanted to know." He looked a bit puzzled and I added, "I was interested in whether Shaw had written any other books, that's all. Trying to fill in his literary background, if any."

"I see. ... Well, I should think he might have done others, but he didn't send any more to me, thank heaven. The poor chap hadn't a clue when it came to putting his ideas down. ... So you're planning to tell the whole story again, are you?"

"I thought I would," I said. "It's a fascinating case."

"Amazing case!" Dancy said. "I didn't know Galloway well myself—I always avoid fellow writers if possible—but he had the reputation of being a pretty stout chap. Wonderful storyteller, too—he must have been off his head to do what he did. I'll never believe it was really necessary. ..." He moved toward the door. "Well, if I'm going to drive my fiancée's battlewagon into Sussex today I suppose I'd better get cracking. ..."

"I hope I haven't held you up too much," I said. "It was decent of you to see me."

"Not a bit." He grinned. "Come again, and interview me about my books. I could do with a bit of free publicity in the *Post*!"

He opened the door, and the Scotties at once launched a fresh offensive. We plowed our way through them and Dancy shook hands with me and said would I mind letting myself out. I patted the dogs, said good-by to Miss Hewitt, and made my way downstairs. There was a telephone box on the other side of the square and I went slowly across to phone Mary.

Chapter Ten

At half past ten that night I drove over to Kew again. I'd told Mary that I'd call round after work and bring the new Shaw exhibits along for her to see, and she was waiting for me. She said "Hullo" in a noncommittal voice and I followed her upstairs to the sitting room. Her face, as she turned, wore its former look of careful indifference. She had herself so well in hand it wasn't human. We were right back where we'd started.

I showed her Dancy's letter, which I'd already read to her over the phone, and opened up Shaw's things. She examined everything very carefully, without commenting. Then she got herself a cigarette and lit it and sat down.

"Well," she said, "I still don't accept it. I"ll never accept it."

I think, in the back of my mind, it was the reaction I'd expected—and feared.

"But, Mary," I said, "you've got to, now—there's no way out at all. Surely you can see that? You've got to, for your own sake. You'll make your life a misery if you go on kicking against the facts as they are."

"If Daddy's going to spend the rest of his days in prison," she said, "my life's going to be a misery anyway." She said it without self-pity, as though it were a self-evident truth.

"That depends on you," I said. "Look, darling, I know how you feel about your father and I know how dreadfully unhappy you are, but it's no good fighting this thing any more. Honestly it isn't. You've simply got to adjust yourself to the situation."

She shook her head. "That's what I can't do. If I thought Daddy had really done what they say, I'd adjust all right. It would be a different problem then. But *I don't think he did.* I'll never think so. I think that somehow or other, in a way I can't begin to understand or explain, he's got himself caught up in a ghastly mess that isn't his fault, and he's going to spend the rest of his life in a cell for something he hasn't done. It's a terrible, shocking injustice. He's only fifty—so alive, so vital. And he's being shut up—for *ever!* How can I reconcile myself to that when I *know* he's done nothing to deserve it?"

"But the evidence, Mary . . ."

"The evidence is *wrong!*"

There was a little silence.

"All right," I said at last, "if you must believe that, you must. But at least you needn't stay here alone, brooding over what's happened. If you can't adjust, then it's all the more reason why you should find something to occupy yourself."

"Oh, don't worry about that," she said. "I shall get a job now. I'll manage."

"If only you wouldn't try to carry the whole thing yourself!" I said. "It's too much of a load for anyone."

"I don't see how I can share it."

"You could if you married me," I said.

She gave a short laugh. "And live happily ever after? What a hope!"

"I'm serious, Mary."

"Then you must be out of your mind. You believe my father is a cheat and a liar and a murderer, and you want to marry me?"

"Yes, I do."

"It's very generous of you!"

"Oh, Mary, don't be so bitter. You know it isn't like that. It's just that, whatever your father may or may not have done, it doesn't alter *you*. I told you before, I love you. I love you just as you are, as I know you, and that's all I care about."

"You're sorry for me," she said.

"Of course I'm sorry for you—who wouldn't be? I want to help you—but it isn't generosity, it's selfishness. Don't you realize that from the very first moment we met you've meant absolutely everything to me? I did try to forget you, for a little while—but it didn't work. You've become my life. I need you—I need to see you and talk to you. I want you around. Always."

She didn't say anything. She just sat curled up in her chair with her head turned away. It was some time before I realized that she was crying. I'd never seen her cry—I would scarcely have believed she could. Once she'd started she couldn't stop. I went over to her and put my arms round her and held her close and tried to comfort her, but there wasn't much I could do except wait.

When at last she spoke to me again, all the hardness had gone from her. "I'm sorry, Peter," she said, "I haven't really wanted to be so beastly to you. You've been so kind and I owe you so much."

"You don't owe me a thing," I said. "Anything I've done I've done for myself, because I love you. . . . Marry me, Mary! For both our sakes. I think in the end I could help you to be happy again—and that would make me happy. At least I'd try very hard."

She was sitting very close to me, holding my hand, and she went on sitting like that for quite a while. She seemed lost in thought. Presently she gave a little sigh and looked up at me sadly.

"Peter," she said, "I was in love with you—of course I was. . . . I expect I still am. I wanted us to marry. It was all so wonderful . . . But now we've got to be sensible. It's no good thinking of marriage any more. You say we could share this thing, but that's just what we can't do. We might if we both looked at it in the same way, but we don't. We're on opposite sides. Imagine living together, year after year, when you thought my father was a murderer and I knew he wasn't! What possible sympathy could there be between us? We couldn't stand it, either of us."

"We wouldn't have to go on discussing it," I said.

"No, but the barrier would always be there—we'd always be conscious of it. . . . And that's not all—suppose we had children? According to you, their grandfather would be a murderer. Doesn't that terrify you?"

"No. If people stopped having children because their parents had behaved badly, the world wouldn't last long."

"Well, it terrifies me. I'd always be afraid you were watching for some horrible trait to come out. . . . You'd probably imagine things, even if they weren't there. I couldn't bear it."

"I'm sure I wouldn't do that," I said. "Why don't I imagine I see horrible traits in you? You have some of your father's genes, after all—you must be like him in some respects. But when I look at you, all I see is something very lovely and very loyal and very brave. If we had children I should see you in them, not your father."

She shook her head. "That's what you think now, Peter, but it might not work out like that. There'd be dynamite around, always. There'd be no peace of mind for either of us. . . . Besides, I don't think it would be fair to have children. What would we tell them? Nothing?—keep it all a dark secret, which they'd be sure to find out in the end? Pretend I was going off to see a friend every time I visited the prison?—that could go on for twenty years, you know. Surely you can see that it's impossible. If you've already got children when a thing like this hits you, you just have to make the best of it—but if you haven't, you've no right to start. That's how it seems to me, anyhow."

I said, "We wouldn't *have* to have children."

"What's marriage without children? If we didn't, and it was because of me, you'd probably finish up by hating me. . . . Peter, you're wrong, I'm sure you are. What we feel about each other now is beside the point. I love you, and I know you love me because you've shown it, and I know we'd both make a great effort—but it wouldn't work. If we married, it would be a broken-backed affair from the beginning. . . . I simply don't believe there's any possibility of happiness for us together."

I got up. "Well," I said, "I don't agree, but if you feel like that there's obviously no point in discussing it any more at the moment. Perhaps you'll see things differently as time goes on."

"It would be better if you didn't think so, Peter—I can't see how the situation can alter. I shan't marry at all—and you'll be far better off with someone else. Write me off, Peter—don't just stick around hoping things will change. It's not fair to yourself."

"That's for me to decide," I said.

Chapter Eleven

I saw nothing at all of Mary during the next week. For the first few days I was out of town on a story, and by the time I got back she'd started putting out feelers about a new secretarial job and was busy seeing people in the mornings, which was usually the only time I was free. I kept in touch with her by phone and she was quite friendly and told me what she was doing and how she was getting on, but when I tried to make a date with her for the weekend she stalled and I couldn't pin her down.

Frustration over Mary was quite enough to keep me milling over the Galloway case. The way things were, it seemed pretty clear that my affair with her was just about through. She'd made up her mind, and I didn't think I'd be able to change it, unless there was a change in the Galloway situation. I kept telling myself that the case was all over now, that there wasn't a loophole left, that dwelling on it was just a waste of energy—but I couldn't let it alone. It worried me that Mary hadn't been able to accept the evidence. Blind faith against the weight of facts was pretty stupid—and Mary was anything but stupid. It wasn't as though she'd had even the glimmer of a doubt. I found it most disturbing. She'd even succeeded in communicating a little of her feeling to me—enough, at least, to make me wish I'd known Galloway myself so that I could have formed my own impression. But it was too late for that now—talking to him through a grille wouldn't be any help.

For several days I continued to go over the rat run of the evidence. I looked at the case again from every angle. My earlier inquiries had been based on the assumption that if Galloway hadn't stolen

Shaw's plot he probably hadn't murdered him either. Now I tried another approach. Even though Galloway *had* stolen Shaw's plot, that didn't necessarily mean he'd murdered him. The evidence for the first was conclusive; the evidence for the second might still, conceivably, be got round. The crucial question, of course, was one which sooner or later Mary and I would have to face in any event—if Galloway hadn't killed Shaw, who had? The answer to that was a blank. As the prosecution had said, there were no other suspects on the horizon. That might be because no one had made any serious attempt to look for any. The defense lawyers would scarcely have known where to start. The police had been convinced from the beginning that they'd got the guilty man so they wouldn't have bothered. Or, more likely, it was because there just weren't any. Certainly nothing had emerged from my own inquiries to suggest that anyone else might have wanted to kill Shaw. Apart from his attitude to Galloway he'd appeared to be the most inoffensive of men. So why should anyone else have attacked him on the towpath?

There was only one way to get an answer to that—assuming there was an answer—and that was to make a new and more exhaustive check on Shaw's relationships with other people. As soon as I got back to town I drew up a list of the more obvious things to look into. There was the possibility that Shaw had been involved with some woman and through her had come up against some man. There was the possibility that he'd been on bad terms with his sister's errant husband. And there was the possibility that the two people who'd overheard the quarrel on the boat had not been just casual passers-by. I didn't think any of the ideas held out much promise, but in a last-ditch struggle long odds were inevitable. At least I wouldn't be giving Mary up without a fight.

Next morning, therefore, I called again on Mrs. Green. I thanked her for the parcel she'd sent me and pressed a small additional check on her. Then I began to probe as tactfully as I could into the more personal aspects of her late brother's life, pretending I wanted the information so that I could give a more rounded picture of him in the book I was planning. But my duplicity got me nowhere.

Of course, said Mrs. Green, Robert *could* have had a girl friend and kept quiet about her, but he'd never seemed very much interested in the opposite sex and he'd certainly never dropped a hint about anyone to her. As for making enemies, I gathered that he'd never had a stand-up quarrel with anyone in his life until he'd met John Galloway. Mrs. Green made him sound almost as colorless as she was herself. I asked her how he'd got on with her husband, and she said the two of them hadn't had much in common because her husband had been rather wild and Robert had been quiet and conventional. Robert had taken a poor view of her husband going off the way he had and leaving his family, but she didn't think there'd been any words between them. I said I'd rather like to talk to her husband, in case he had another angle on Robert, and would she mind telling me where I could find him, and she gave me his address. Apparently he lived and worked at Slough, where he was some sort of engineer.

I couldn't get to Slough that day but in the evening I was sent to cover a political meeting at Twickenham and that gave me a chance to take a look at Donald Thorpe, the towpath witness. At his house, which I reached just before ten, I was told he was at the pictures with his fiancée and would be taking her home afterward, so I drove to her address in Surbiton and waited outside in the car until they showed up. The light wasn't good in the road and I couldn't see them very clearly but what I could see was prepossessing. Thorpe was a dark-haired, good-looking young man of husky build and the girl an exceptionally pretty blonde. She turned out to be the Anita Robinson who'd been with him the night Shaw had been killed. I apologized for troubling them at such a late hour and told my story about writing up the Shaw case. They were both quite friendly and ready enough to talk, but now that I'd seen them I'd rather lost interest. They seemed a straightforward pair and I couldn't believe there'd been anything sinister about their towpath walk. I took them quickly through the quarrel incident again and then drove back to town.

I was on day duty next day, which meant that by seven in the evening I was free to go in search of Mrs. Green's husband at

Slough. I found him eventually in a pub near his lodgings, drinking beer with a couple of cronies. He was a formidable-looking chap, with heavy shoulders and a swarthy, scowling face. At least, it scowled at me when I told him what I wanted. He'd had enough beer to make him difficult and he couldn't see why I should want to know so much about Shaw even if I was writing up the case. I paid for a round of drinks and managed to smooth him down and finally got a franker view about Shaw than I'd expected. According to Green, he'd been a "prissy little runt" and not a man at all. Clever, Green said, in a sly way, but bloodless, like his sister. Not that Green had known him well, but he hadn't wanted to—it had been the mistake of his life ever to get mixed up with that family. He spoke with contempt for Shaw, rather than dislike, and I couldn't imagine he'd ever have troubled to quarrel with him. When I mentioned the possibility of a woman in Shaw's life, Green gave a guffaw that shook the pub. I left shortly before closing time, having got precisely nowhere.

By now I'd exhausted my list of people to question. If I tried, I could probably dig up some more contacts, but I felt far from encouraged. The only result of my inquiries had been to make it seem even more unlikely that any of Shaw's acquaintances would have felt strongly enough about him to kill him. There was, perhaps, an outside chance that he might have been attacked by a complete stranger, some towpath thug, but it seemed highly improbable, particularly as there'd been no suggestion of robbery—and in any case there was nothing I could do about that. I drove home in a very dejected frame of mind.

It was after eleven when I reached the flat. I'd have liked to ring Mary, if only to hear the sound of her voice, but I remembered that she'd have to go downstairs to answer the phone and it seemed a bit late to disturb the houee for a chat. Instead, I had a bath and turned in with a book. But I couldn't read. I lay in bed with the light on, thinking about Mary, thinking about Galloway and the mess he'd made of her life and his own, thinking how unnecessary it had all been, thinking what an extraordinary aberration it had been for him to risk stealing someone else's plot when he was such a competent storyteller himself. . . . It took a bit of understanding. In fact, if there hadn't been so much evidence it would have been quite unbelievable. My thoughts switched to the defense plea at the trial—the plea of coincidence. They could never have thought they had much hope of getting away with it, yet I could see why they'd chosen it—they'd had nothing else. And, of course, chance *was* an odd thing. It was said that if enough monkeys hammered on enough typewriters for long enough, they'd produce all Shakespeare's plays. One didn't have to go as far into fantasy as that to suppose that Galloway and Shaw, working separately, might have hammered out the same plot. But still too far for credibility. The nearest the defense had come to making their plea credible was when they'd suggested that both men might, unwittingly, have drawn the plot from the same source. Suppose they had both come across the original, years ago, in the same book and forgotten all about it? Shaw, at least, must have read pretty well everything in the thriller line that had ever been published. . . .

I glanced across at the great pile of thrillers still stacked against the wall. It was absurd, I thought—it would be a complete waste of time to look through them. But time was something I didn't value very much at the moment and I certainly had a unique opportunity to discover just what Shaw *had* read. . . . I got out of bed and pulled up a chair and started to go systematically through the pile. Shaw had evidently been an assiduous buyer at secondhand shops, for quite a lot of the hard-cover books were old titles that had been published in the twenties and thirties, and many of the paperbacks were pretty ancient too. I took them as they came. Some I could set aside at once because I'd read them, and remembered what they were about. Most of the paperbacks had a short summary of the plot on the cover. Where there wasn't a summary, it needed little more than a glance inside to tell me what the plot was about. In the course of half an hour or so I found two with sea themes and one with a diving background, but naturally they had no relation to the Shaw-Galloway plot.

I was about three-quarters of the way through the pile when I noticed the corner of a photograph protruding from one of the books, and pulled it out. It was a head-and-shoulders portrait of a well-set-up young man in his middle twenties, good-looking in a rather tough way, with darkish hair and a dark hairline mustache. Oddly enough, I had a feeling that I'd seen him somewhere, but I couldn't place him. I wondered if he was well-known, because it was a glossy picture, the sort generally used for press reproduction. I turned it over and there was a name on the back—Grant Fresher. It didn't mean anything to me. The name was written in ink but it didn't look like a signature—it looked more like a record made by a filing clerk. In fact, the whole picture reminded me of photographs I'd seen in the Art Library at the *Post*. I had another look at the face and it certainly seemed familiar. What was more, I had a notion I'd seen it very recently, while I'd been making my inquiries about Shaw. It was some young man I'd met in the last day or two. . . . At once, I thought of Donald Thorpe. It *could* be he. I hadn't seen his face very clearly, I didn't even know whether he'd had a hairline mustache or not, but the type of face was certainly the same.

It was an exciting idea. Perhaps, after all, I'd been hasty in dismissing Thorpe from the case after ten minutes' conversation in the dark. If he and Shaw *had* been acquainted before the murder, the possibilities were limitless. They could have been deeply involved with each other in a dozen different ways. Thorpe's girl friend could have been involved too. The impression of youthful innocence that she and Thorpe had given me might have been completely phony. That towpath stroll of theirs might, after all, have been sinister. But there wasn't much point in speculating until I'd taken another look at Thorpe and checked whether he really was the man in the picture. I decided I'd drive down first thing in the morning and try and catch him before he left for work.

With so much on my mind I slept fitfully, and I was glad when daylight came. I rose at six, brewed myself some coffee, and left just after seven for Teddington. By a quarter to eight I was parked outside Thorpe's house, waiting for him to come out. I didn't think I'd need to speak to him—one look would be enough to tell me whether he was the man I hoped he was, and after that I could make my plans at leisure. I didn't have to wait long. At five past eight the front door opened and he came out smartly. He paused to open the gate, giving me a good view of his face—and I saw with a pang of disappointment that he wasn't the man in the picture. The style was the same, but the features were quite different. Despondently, I started the engine and set off back to town.

The first thing I did when I reached the flat was to take another look at the picture. I thought perhaps I'd been imagining things, but I hadn't. It *did* remind me of someone, most strongly. Perhaps, I thought, it was of someone I'd seen in the course of my Shaw inquiries, but not in connection with them. I wished I could place the man, because if I couldn't it was bound to nag at me. I cooked some breakfast and read through the *Post* and then I went and had another look at the picture. It was, I decided, the expression of the eyes that was familiar, but I still didn't know who it was.

I had a free day ahead and no special plans for filling it. After breakfast I went into the bedroom to clear up the books which were still scattered about the floor. There weren't many now that I hadn't looked at and I thought I might as well finish the job I'd started. I squatted down among the litter and began to work my way through the last pile. I'd almost got to the end when, as I turned the flyleaf of a rather tattered volume, my eye was caught by the name of the author—*Grant Fresher*. So Fresher was a writer—one I hadn't heard of—and this, presumably, was the book I'd pulled the photograph out of, since the two things clearly went together. The title of the book was *The Black Hat*. It was a stiff-covered, secondhand book, which Shaw had apparently bought for ninepence. I paged through it, but its theme wasn't anything to do with underwater diving. It was a tough gangster story, a bit sexy. I looked to see when it had been published, and the year was 1934.

Suddenly, it occurred to me that if the book was twenty years old, the photograph might be twenty years old, too—in which case Fresher might well look very different now. It seemed quite likely, because men didn't wear hairline mustaches much nowadays. I went to the photograph again and covered up the mustache and curved my hand experimentally round the top of Fresher's head to hide the youthful hair—and at once I knew whom it reminded me of.

Richard Dancy!

I was enormously intrigued—but cautious. I'd made one mistake about the picture already that day. It didn't *have* to be Dancy, I told myself, just because it reminded me of him. Lots of people looked a bit like each other. . . . I delved among the heap of paperback thrillers and found one by Dancy, with a picture of him on the back cover. It didn't help much. The look in the eyes was the same, but that was all. Dancy's face was much plumper, his mouth tighter. I could easily be deceiving myself. But if I wasn't, it was a fascinating find. Dancy had said that Shaw had been a stranger to him. That could still be true, of course. Shaw could have bought this book secondhand with the photograph already in it—a photograph left by some earlier fan of Fresher's, perhaps—without having any idea that it was of Dancy. But if the picture had belonged to a fan, why wasn't it properly autographed? If it hadn't, where had it come from? Wasn't it, in any case, rather a coincidence that Shaw should have had in his possession an old, unrecognized photograph of Dancy by another name, and that Dancy should have been one of the three authors he'd picked on to send his manuscript to?

I thought about it for a while. I couldn't see anything very clearly. I certainly didn't jump to any lightning conclusions. All I knew was that there were a lot of questions in my mind and that I'd like to find out more about Grant Fresher. I looked to see who had published *The Black Hat* and it was a well-known firm named Gale & McGhee, who had their office in St. James's. Twenty minutes later I was on my way to see them.

Chapter Twelve

I had no appointment, and it took me a little time to find anyone at Gale & McGhee's who could tell me anything at all. I saw a secretary, who passed me on to a young man, who looked at my copy of *The Black Hat* and said he was sorry, he'd never even heard of Fresher himself, but perhaps Mr. Cogan, the senior partner, would be able to help me, only he was busy at the moment and would I care to hang on? I said I would and he disappeared with the book and I waited. It was nearly eleven when I was finally shown into Cogan's office. The senior partner was a distinguished-looking man, white-haired and sixtyish, with an Edwardian charm of manner.

He shook hands and motioned me to a chair. He had my copy of *The Black Hat* on the desk in front of him. "Well, now, Mr. Rennie," he said, "I understand you've been making inquiries about Grant Fresher?"

"Yes," I said. "I wondered if you could tell me who he is and how I could get hold of him. That is, if it's not a publishing secret!"

Cogan looked at me curiously. "May I ask why you're interested?"

"Of course ... The thing is, I'm planning to write up the Shaw murder case—you remember, John Galloway ..."

"I do, indeed."

"Well, I've been going through some of Shaw's documents, checking up on his interests and his contacts, and I found this photograph of Fresher among his belongings...." I passed it across.

Cogan took it and looked at it for a moment and then he glanced at me again, a bit quizzically. "That's right," he said. "I gave this photograph to Shaw myself about two years ago."

I stared at him. "*You* did!"

"Yes—I gave it to him when he called here one day, exactly as you've done, to ask about Fresher. Odd, isn't it? He even brought this same copy of *The Black Hat* with him."

I felt completely at sea. I said, "Why was *he* interested?"

"He said he was writing a monograph on what he called 'the early tough school' of English crime fiction, and he'd just read an old book by a man named Grant Fresher which we'd published and which came into the category, and he wondered if we could give him any information about the author. ... Well, sometimes we can, of course, and sometimes we can't. In this case, I didn't feel particularly keen, but Shaw was rather pressing, and he was a librarian, and we always like to oblige librarians when we can! So in the end I told him what I could, and he was very much interested and asked if we had a picture of Fresher, and our publicity people hunted about in their files and managed to dig up this photograph."

"Yes, I see. ... Well, may I know what you told Shaw?"

Cogan smiled. "I don't see why not, Mr. Rennie—we like to oblige newspapermen, too, and it's all old history now. Anyhow, these are the facts. Fresher did three books for us, back in the early thirties. They were on the tough side, but they were quite well written, and we were happy to publish them because we were trying hard to build up a thriller list at the time and Fresher was a young man and we thought he probably had a future. The books didn't set the Thames on fire but they sold fairly well considering that his name wasn't known. Then he brought us a fourth manuscript. This time it wasn't just tough—it was so nearly pornographic that we had no alternative but to turn it down flat. And that was the whole extent of our dealings with Mr. Fresher."

"What happened to him?" I asked.

"Well, he found another publisher. I can't remember the fellow's name—he was quite disreputable, anyway. The book that we'd rejected was published, and somehow it got by the police. The next one didn't. Fresher and the publisher were both prosecuted for obscene libel, and if I remember rightly they got twelve months apiece. And that's really all I can tell you."

"You don't know what happened to Fresher when he came out of prison?"

"I've no idea at all. I'm afraid I wasn't very much interested."

"No," I said, "I can understand that. . . . Anyway, what sort of a man was he? What sort of impression did you have of him when you were publishing him?"

"Well, it's a long time ago, Mr. Rennie, and my recollections are a little vague. . . . I know I didn't care for him a great deal, but then there are many authors one doesn't terribly care for! He was, if I remember, rather a tough young man himself—he was mixed up with the Blackshirt movement, and used to act as a bodyguard at meetings. . . . Not a very attractive type, I'm afraid."

"Was the name 'Grant Fresher' a pseudonym? It sounds like it."

"I imagine it was, but it was the only name I ever knew him by."

"Did he have an agent?"

"No, he dealt with us direct. He used to write from some address in Hampstead, but of course that's twenty years ago and he must have moved on. Anyway, we've no record of him now—it was pure chance that we still had his photograph."

"I'm rather surprised that Shaw wanted it," I said, "after he'd heard your account."

"I was a bit surprised myself, but then he was a strange little man. He seemed to think it had historical value, and we certainly had no use for it ourselves. . . ." Cogan regarded me shrewdly. "You must be going into Shaw's affairs in great detail, Mr. Rennie, if you're following up every document with such care. I'd scarcely have thought he was worth a long biography."

I didn't rise to that. Earlier, I'd been prepared to put my cards on the table and explain that Fresher's picture had reminded me of someone else and that that was why I was interested. Now it seemed wiser not to.

"It's just my newspaper training," I said with a smile. "We're supposed to be thorough!" I took the book that Cogan was holding out to me, and picked up Fresher's picture. "Anyhow, thank you very much indeed for helping me."

Chapter Thirteen

I left the building in a state of simmering excitement. The possible implications of what I'd learned were startling. The Galloway case might well have taken an entirely new turn that morning. But everything depended on what was still no more than a suspicion—that Grant Fresher and Richard Dancy were in fact one and the same man. Before I launched out on a sea of speculation I had to satisfy myself of that. What was more I had to be in a position to prove it to others.

I had a quick lunch and then went along to the office. I knew no better place than the *Post's* library for starting an identity check and I spent most of the afternoon there, going through old cuttings and reference books. My idea was that if I worked backward from Dancy and forward from Fresher, I might find some connecting link in the middle. But it didn't work out like that. Dancy's personal file proved to be extremely thin and gave no real picture of him at all. He didn't appear to have carved out any special niche for himself in the thriller-writing business and he'd scarcely been mentioned by the gossip writers. He'd managed to get himself a bit of publicity at the time of the Mystery Guild exhibition and he'd taken part in a symposium on crime writing in the *Gazette* a few months ago, but that was about all. The reference books were hardly more informative. Even the *Authors' Who's Who* had no more than half a dozen lines on him, naming a few of his books and giving his publisher and his London address and his favorite recreation—fishing.

The Grant Fresher material was more interesting but equally unhelpful. Fresher had operated too long ago to appear in any of the reference books, but I managed to find some cuttings about him in an old file. There were several paragraphs about his early books, including a favorable mention of *The Black Hat*, and three separate reports of the twenty-year-old obscenity case, with a couple of bad photographs of him that seemed to me to resemble neither Dancy nor the picture of Fresher that I'd seen. The name of the publisher who'd been jailed with Fresher was given as James Evershed Cullis and I looked him up in the various directories but found nothing. He, too, no doubt, had changed his name. As far as the library's resources were concerned, the Fresher trial ended with the verdict. My hopes of a link simply hadn't materialized.

There were several courses still open to me. The longest and most laborious would be a personal investigation of Dancy's life, tracing his movements and activities back through the years with the help of people who'd known him. That might or might not be productive. The short cut would be to get hold of his fingerprints somehow and have them checked at the Criminal Records Office, where Fresher's prints would probably still be on file—but that would be difficult to organize and might get me into trouble. So far I'd nothing at all on Dancy except an expression in the eye, and unless I moved cautiously I might find myself at the wrong end of a slander action. An intermediate possibility would be to try and get Dancy and the publisher, Cogan, to some meeting place and see if Cogan could identify him as Fresher—but that would be tricky, too. In the end I decided my best initial step was to see Dancy again myself and do a little preliminary probing. I could manage that, easily if not ethically, by telling him I'd like to interview him for the *Post* as he himself had suggested.

I went down to the Reporters' Room and tried to get him on the phone right away, but there was no reply from his flat. It was Friday, and I wondered if he'd gone down to spend the weekend with his fiancée in the country. It seemed worth a try. I looked up her number in the Sussex directory and put a call in. The address was Sanctuary, Old Stone Lane, Clooden, near Lewes. Lavinia answered the phone herself. I recalled our earlier meeting and said I was rather anxious to get in touch with Mr. Dancy, and she said that would be easy because he was sitting right beside her. My luck was in. A moment later he came on the line. I explained that I'd like to interview him and he was delighted and asked me when I could come. I thought quickly. I was on duty the next day, Saturday, but free on Sunday. I said would it be all right if I drove down on Sunday morning. He said that Sunday afternoon would be better because he and Lavinia would probably be at church in the morning. We finally settled for three o'clock.

It was an extraordinary place that Lavinia Hewitt had. Clooden turned out to be miles from anywhere—the "near Lewes" in the phone book was just a thundering lie—and Old Stone Lane proved to be a dangerously eroded track that almost bounced me out of my car. The house itself was a small and quite hideous red brick bungalow, set in what appeared to be an endless expanse of wasteland. The "sanctuary" part of the address presumably referred solely to animals, for humanly speaking the place looked scarcely habitable. Poles and wire netting rose up on all sides, dividing the immediate surroundings of the house into separate compounds for dogs, cats, goats, an aviary, some donkeys and a horse. I parked my car beside Lavinia's ancient station wagon and a slightly more reputable Austin, which I assumed was Dancy's, and made my way past a row of kennels to the front door. Inside the small porch there was a wooden box with some literature in it about vivisection and cruelty to old horses in North Africa, and an invitation to "Help Yourself." Above the door, a slogan informed me that "There Is No Welfare State for Animals." I was about to press the bell when a big healthy-looking girl emerged from the side of the house with a pail in her hand and called out to me above the noise of barking dogs that Miss Hewitt was "round the back." I went round and found Lavinia and Dancy sitting in deck chairs on a scrubby bit of grass that evidently passed for lawn. Lavinia, in a curious sort of smock and gum boots, looked even more eccentric than when I'd seen her before. She shook hands and Dancy gave me what I thought was a slightly sheepish grin and after a few polite exchanges I got down to the business of the interview.

I started with the routine stuff—how many books Dancy had written and how long it took him to write them and what hours he worked and so on. He said he'd done about fifteen books and they'd all been published by the same publisher and had been moderately successful. He'd also written a lot of short stories as well. I asked him what he'd done before he became a writer and he said he'd been in the Army all through the war, in the Royal Engineers, and before that he'd knocked around the world, doing a bit of farming and a bit of oil drilling—chiefly with the idea of getting interesting experiences to write about later, because he'd always wanted to write. He talked well and easily, and all the time Lavinia beamed at him fondly. I asked him where he'd been to school and he said in Sydney, New South Wales—he'd been born in Australia and had come to England as a young man. I said that was a reversal of the normal procedure and he said yes, but he preferred England, he thought it was a grand country and he couldn't stand people who tried to run it down. I asked him if he'd ever been interested in politics and he said no. I touched on his hobbies and said I understood he was a keen fisherman and he grinned and said he'd done a lot of trout fishing in Wales, but he didn't know what was going to happen about that now because Lavinia thought fishing was a cruel sport. I moved on from there to his current plans and asked Lavinia when they expected to get married and she said at Christmas and proceeded to tell me about their "romance." Apparently they'd met about a year earlier and all because of her animals. Dancy had needed some background material about the boarding of animals for one of his books, and a society had put him in touch with Lavinia, who was one of their stalwarts. As a result he'd become fond not only of Lavinia but of animals too, and when they were married they hoped to develop the "Sanctuary" into a much larger establishment I asked Lavinia if she'd always lived at Clooden and she said yes, but not in this bungalow—her father had had a house called "The Gables," where she'd kept a horse and a few dogs, but after he'd died three years ago she'd moved here because there was more land and plenty of room for expansion.

Presently she excused herself and went in to make tea. I continued to prod away at Dancy for a bit, but I knew I wasn't getting very far. He had an air of being very forth-coming about everything, but he'd scarcely given me a single fact that I could check. I watched him all the time as he talked and in spite of the plump face and the jovial grin I still thought I could detect a likeness to the Fresher picture. Fresher had been dark, of course, and Dancy with his bald head and rosy cheeks gave a general impression of pinkness, but now that I was able to look at him more closely I saw that his chin and upper lip were blue-shaved. As a young man, he'd have been dark, too. And he was about the right age. Suddenly I decided to put the matter to the test. It might work, and I'd nothing to lose.

"You know," I said, "I was rather surprised to hear that you'd never used a pseudonym. I had the idea that you'd once written under the name of Grant Fresher."

His pale blue stare transfixed me. I'd caught him utterly off guard—his gaze showed much more than the mild inquiry that would have been natural if Fresher had meant nothing to him. In that moment of revelation I knew that I'd been right.

He quickly recovered himself, and tried to bluff it out. "Grant Fresher?" he said. "Never heard of him. Who's he?"

I produced Fresher's picture and showed it to him. He looked at it for a moment in a puzzled way. Then he said, "I don't get it—you're not suggesting I'm like this chap, are you?"

"It struck me there was a resemblance," I said. I caught the chink of crockery on a tray as Lavinia emerged from the bungalow. "Let's see what your fiancée thinks."

He stared at me for a second. Then he suddenly said in an urgent whisper, "Put it away!" and winked violently and put his finger to his lips. I slipped the picture back into my pocket.

Lavinia put the tray down and said, "Well, have you two finished your interview?" and Dancy said, "Yes, I think Mr. Rennie's got pretty well all he needs now," and gave me another collusive wink. Lavinia poured the tea and for the next twenty minutes we talked solidly about cats. After that she insisted on showing me round the whole place. It was Dancy who said at last, "Well, I expect you'd like to be getting along, Rennie." I agreed that it was about time and he said he'd walk down to the gate with me.

I said good-by to Lavinia and followed Dancy through the maze of wire netting to the car. As soon as we were out of sight of the house he stopped and gripped my arm. He had a grip like iron but he was friendly enough.

"Look, I'm sorry about all that," he said, "but you had me properly scared. ... Where on earth did you get that picture?"

"It was among Robert Shaw's things," I said. "Remember—the Galloway case man."

"Really ...? Now how the devil would he have got it?"

I shrugged. "He collected old thrillers—I found it in a Grant Fresher book called *The Black Hat*.''

"And you thought it was like me?"

"It is like you," I said.

He nodded grimly. "Well, now, look here, old boy—I'm going to ask you to do me a big favor and forget all about it. I'll tell you why. I *was* Grant Fresher, and I did a damn stupid thing. I wrote a couple of smutty books—sort of literary wild oats, you know. You're a man of the world, I'm a man of the world—these things do happen. ... I was pretty young at the time and I've often regretted it since. Anyway I got into a bit of trouble with the police—nothing much, but I was hauled up before the beaks and fined. It's all forgotten now—I've been a respectable citizen for twenty years. But my fiancée's rather strait-laced—fine woman, you know, bit religious and all that. I'd hate her to know about it—I can tell you I was really shaken, up there at the house. ... So if you could just forget the whole thing I'd be enormously obliged. What do you say?"

"But of course," I said. I didn't challenge his version—I'd got his identity confirmed and that for the moment was all that mattered. "I certainly don't want to make any trouble—it was just that I was intrigued by the resemblance. Don't worry—Miss Hewitt won't hear anything about it from me."

"That's very decent of you, old boy." He seized my hand and

shook it heartily. "Very decent of you indeed. . . ." He grinned. "If you ever want to board a dog I'll see it's put up at a reduced rate! Good-by."

Chapter Fourteen

I scarcely noticed the journey back to town. I was too busy dreaming up a dramatic new theory.

Until this Fresher business had come to light I'd had no reason to doubt Dancy's good faith in the Shaw affair. I'd accepted him as an independent and reputable writer whose letter to Shaw, reinforcing Blundell's, had virtually put paid to any possibility of Galloway's innocence. But now, with the Fresher-Dancy identity established, his credit as a witness was badly shaken. He'd been a crook twenty years ago and he might still be a crook. If he was, he could have had a crooked tie-up with Shaw. He could have teamed up with Shaw in a plot to frame Galloway for money, and a phony, predated letter from him, written to collaborate one from Blundell that Shaw had already faked, could have been his contribution. Later, there could have been a quarrel, and Dancy could have murdered Shaw!

There was an alternative possibility, a variation. Dancy's association with Shaw could have been a forced one. Shaw might well have discovered that Fresher was Dancy, just as I had. He'd known about Fresher's prison record, which would have given him a hold over Dancy. He might have blackmailed him into writing the letter. Blackmail would have been in line with Shaw's tendencies, and it was a powerful motive for murder. But on reflection I doubted if a threat to expose a twenty-year-old prison record would have sufficed to bring a tough customer like Dancy to heel. Whom would Shaw have threatened to tell? The obvious answer seemed to be Lavinia, in view of Dancy's sharp reaction to the possibility of her learning the truth about him. Yet I found it hard to believe that

Dancy was so attached to Lavinia that he'd have submitted to blackmail because of her. He might be, of course, even though she was so dreadfully unattractive. He certainly gave every appearance of being devoted. It was a curious engagement, altogether. I wondered if by any chance Lavinia had a bit of money tucked away somewhere. She hadn't given that impression, with her dowdy clothes and decrepit car and ugly little bungalow, but you could never tell with these eccentric spinsters. It was definitely worth looking into.

There was nothing I could do about it on a Sunday, but sharp at nine next morning I drove round to Somerset House to check up on Lavinia's father's will. If there was money in the family, there should be some indication of it there. I had all the information I needed to get the will traced and in a few minutes the file was brought to me. I paid my inspection fee and turned up the details.

For a moment I could scarcely believe my eyes. The figures were enormous. Gross value of the estate, £165,423. Net value, £159,027. Duty paid, £79,543. Fascinated, I ran my eye down the list of bequests. Most of them had been to faithful servants and they were all quite minor until I came to the last one. There was nothing minor about that. "The residue to my daughter, Lavinia Mabel Hewitt, absolutely." The residue! The best part of £80,000!

I closed the file and walked slowly out to the car. The Lavinia-Dancy engagement no longer seemed curious—and the hold I imagined Shaw might have had over Dancy no longer seemed slight. Dancy, obviously, was a fortune hunter. Somehow he'd discovered that Lavinia had money, a lot of money, and he'd gone all out to get her to the altar. Then Shaw had found out that Dancy was Fresher and that he'd been jailed for obscenity. A word in Lavinia's ear would almost certainly have ended the engagement, and the eighty thousand pounds would have been lost. Shaw would have been in a position to dictate terms. Dancy, as I now saw it, *had* been blackmailed.

My theory had been given a tremendous boost, but it still needed a great deal of work done on it. So far it was scarcely more than an outline. Back at the flat, I started to go through the whole case again, looking for facts to fill out the picture. I'd barely begun when I hit a fearful snag. In my eagerness to develop the Shaw-Dancy aspect, I'd completely overlooked a vital batch of old evidence—the parcel of Shaw's effects that Mrs. Green had sent me. At the time, I'd taken those things as conclusive proof that Shaw had thought up his own story. And what was proof then was proof now.

I still had all the stuff in a cupboard. I fished it out and had another look at it. It was horribly convincing. I tried Mary's method, refusing to allow myself to be swayed by mere evidence! If my theory was right, I told myself, these exhibits—whatever the appearance to the contrary—must have been faked. But how? I examined the underwater diving books again. It didn't take me long to decide that they *could* have been faked. Shaw could have bought them after Galloway's book had been published and inserted the marginal comments and cross-references afterward. The same thing applied to the notebook and the draft chapter. There was nothing there that couldn't have been fabricated afterward by a clever and industrious crook. But the newspaper cuttings were a different matter. All but one had the original date of the paper incorporated in the cutting, and the dates preceded the publication of Galloway's book by more than a year. Would Shaw have been able to select and acquire these cuttings twelve months after the papers containing them had appeared? He certainly wouldn't have been able to get much help from the back numbers departments of the newspaper offices themselves after all that time. As a librarian, of course, he might have had access to back files of newspapers—but would he, with his criminal plan in mind, have wanted to cut articles on underwater diving from public files in his own care? I very much doubted it.

The newspaper cuttings had unsettled me and I no longer knew what to think of my Shaw-Dancy theory. Looking at it again with normally skeptical eyes I had to admit that it was almost pure supposition. I knew that Shaw had discovered the truth about Fresher, but I didn't know for certain that he'd identified Fresher with Dancy. Even if he had, I couldn't prove that he'd ever used his knowledge. It was significant, I thought, that he'd been so anxious to hang on to Fresher's photograph—as an instrument of blackmail it would have been invaluable, as a collector's piece it would have been puerile—but significance wasn't proof. I couldn't prove that Shaw had known about Lavinia's fortune. I couldn't prove that Shaw had met Dancy. I certainly couldn't prove that Dancy had killed him. In fact, I couldn't prove a thing. I had a theory which, up to a point, made sense. That was all.

So what was I going to do about it? As things stood, it was hard to see what I could do. I hadn't nearly enough evidence to go to the police and seek their co-operation. With Galloway convicted and sentenced and the case, from their point of view, closed, they'd never take me seriously. I'd have to be much more sure before I could bring them in. But how could I become surer? How could I test my theory? Where could I go for new facts?

I'd been living with the case so long I was beginning to get desperate. I wanted to finish with it, one way or the other. In the end I decided the boldest course was the best. I'd go to the fountainhead. I'd confront Dancy and put my cards on the table. I had one card that might turn out a trump. I'd use that, and see how he reacted. His nerve was probably good—but a guilty man suddenly faced with an accusation of murder might well make some mistake. It seemed the only hope. It would be a tough meeting, but I couldn't see that I'd anything much to lose. The way things were, I'd already lost what I cared about most.

Chapter Fifteen

I called on Dancy at noon the next day, without an appointment. He came down in his shirtsleeves, smoking a pipe. He seemed surprised to see me. I said I'd be glad of a few words with him and he asked me to go up.

"You don't want more stuff for that interview, surely?" he said, as he showed me into his study.

"No, it's not that. . . . As a matter of fact, I'm afraid the interview's off."

"Oh?" He looked disappointed. "Why?"

"The usual thing—change of mind at the top. . . . Perhaps it's just as well, actually—readers are fussy people and some of them have long memories."

He gave me a sharp glance. "I don't get you," he said.

"I checked up on that bit of trouble you had with the police. You weren't exactly frank with me, were you? According to my information, you were given a jail sentence."

There was a little pause. Then he said, "Oh, you found out about that, did you? I thought perhaps you might. . . . Yes, the fact is I had the bad luck to come up against a narrow-minded judge. It should have been a fine, of course."

I said, "It was a pretty bad case, Dancy. I'm not surprised you were so anxious to keep it from Miss Hewitt. It would certainly ruin your chances of marrying her if she got to know about it and I'm sure you wouldn't like that. I understand she's a very wealthy woman!"

I saw the muscles of his forearms tighten. There was a moment of dangerous quiet. Then he said, "You know, I'm beginning not to like you very much, Rennie. In fact, I've a good mind to throw you out on your neck."

"You can't afford to throw me out," I said. "You wouldn't want a big scene and the police brought in, would you? I mean, Miss Hewitt would want to know what the brawl had been about. Then it would probably all come out—about Fresher."

Dancy's pink face grew pinker. "Now look here," he said, "I don't know what your game is, but I can tell you this—if you're thinking of trying a bit of blackmail you've picked the wrong man. It could be very dangerous for you."

"That I can believe!" I said. "But as it happens I'm not thinking of trying a bit of blackmail."

"Then why are you so damned interested in my affairs?"

"I'm interested," I said, "in Shaw and Galloway. I told you—I'm writing up the case."

"What on earth's my past career got to do with Shaw and Galloway?"

"It could have a lot to do with them," I said. "You see, it seems quite possible that it wasn't Galloway who killed Shaw, after all."

He stared at me. "You mean you've found some new ..." He broke off, puzzled. "I still don't see what it's got to do with me."

"It seems quite possible," I said, "that you killed Shaw!"

His jaw dropped, his blue eyes regarded me in wonderment. For a moment he didn't say anything. Then his plump face creased, and he suddenly threw his head back and gave a huge guffaw.

It was most disconcerting. I told myself that a man who could simulate passion for Miss Hewitt could simulate anything, but he looked and sounded genuine enough. He was fairly rocking with laughter. I watched him coldly.

Presently he drew a deep breath and wiped the tears from his eyes. "God," he said, "I haven't had a belly laugh like that in years ...! You mean you came here to accuse me of murder—not to make trouble about Lavinia?"

"That's right."

"Oh dear, oh dear ...!" For a moment I thought he was going

to start all over again. "Well, that's a relief, I must say—now I can relax. . . ." He went to a cupboard. "This calls for a drink, I think."

"Not for me, thanks."

"Oh, come on, old boy, there's no need to be huffy. . . . No? Well, I will, if you don't mind. . . ." He poured himself a glass of sherry. His equanimity seemed completely restored. "You know, the trouble with you newspaper chaps is that you're always trying to make headlines whether the facts justify them or not. . . . Do sit down." He dropped into a chair. "Now tell me, what *is* this extraordinary idea you've got hold of?"

I told him. I didn't accuse him—I just outlined the possible case. I described in detail the frame-up plan that Shaw could have worked out and I explained how Blundell's letter could have been faked. I went on to deal with Shaw's visit to the publisher, his discoveries about Fresher, his possible discovery that Fresher was Dancy, his need of a second letter about his manuscript, his opportunity for blackmail because of Miss Hewitt, and the conceivable outcome on the towpath. As I marshaled the points and developed the argument, it seemed to me that I was making quite a case. Yet I still didn't know whether I believed it or not.

Dancy listened intently till the end—I'd never had a more interested audience. He seemed absolutely fascinated, and I could have sworn it was all new to him. He didn't interrupt me at all, but at the end he slapped his hands together almost with jubilation. "Well, I can tell you one thing," he said. "That would make a first-rate plot for one of my books."

"If it turns out to be true," I said, "it will make an even better plot for someone else's!"

He laughed. "Well, I'm sorry to disappoint you, but I'm afraid it's not true. I'm not exactly a plaster saint, as you've gathered, but I do draw the line at murder. . . . Mind you, it's an incredibly ingenious theory—I hand it to you for working all that out. But the plain truth is, I never met Shaw in my life, so it all falls to the ground."

"The last time we talked," I said, "you told me the plain truth was that you'd been fined for an indiscretion. You sounded most plausible—but the fact was that you'd been jailed for obscenity. Can you really expect me to take your word for anything? I'm afraid I'll have to do quite a bit more checking before I abandon my theory."

His face clouded. "Now see here, Rennie, you'll agree I've taken this nonsense in good part—I've sat here quietly while you've accused me of bashing a man on the head, which some chaps might have resented. I didn't mind, simply because it *was* such nonsense. But if you're going to start talking to other people, it's not going to be long before something leaks out about the Fresher business, and that's a very different matter. My fiancée might hear—and I can't let that happen, you know. You'd better watch your step."

"I'll watch it," I said, "don't worry. But I've gone too far now to turn back."

Alarm showed in his eyes. "You mean you've already talked about this to someone?"

"Not yet," I said, "but I'll have to. ... Unless, of course, you can *prove* in some way that you had nothing to do with the Shaw affair."

"I would if I could," he said, "like a shot—anything to keep you quiet! But how can I?"

I played my one card. "You could tell me where you were the night Shaw was murdered."

"My dear chap, how can I possibly tell?—for one thing, I don't remember when he was murdered. Even if I did, I wouldn't know where I was—it was months ago."

"It was last Easter Saturday," I said. "You ought to know where you were at Easter. Perhaps you were with Miss Hewitt?"

"Easter!" His face suddenly cleared. "Why, of course, I remember now, I was ..." He broke off. "Look, are you planning to check this?"

"I might."

"Then I'm damned if I'm going to tell you. I was with good friends, and I'm not going to have them worried with a lot of slanderous nonsense."

"If I do check," I said, "there'll be no slander. I'll cover up with some harmless story. I'm used to it, you know."

"Is that a promise?"

"It's a promise."

"Right—then this is where you say goodby to your theory. I was in Wales, staying with a couple named Corbett, an artist and his wife. I left London—let me see—about midday on Saturday, and I got there just after dark. And if it's of any interest to you, it rained the whole weekend!"

"Can I get these people on the telephone?"

"No, they don't have one—it's just a cottage on a mountainside, very isolated. They spend all their time painting and fishing. When they want to be sociable they come to London."

"They're not in London now, I suppose?"

"No, they're up in Wales—I heard from Corbett only a fortnight ago. But you're wasting your time, old chap, if you're thinking of going up there. They'll only tell you what I've told you."

"Where is the cottage?" I said.

"It's about four miles from Dolgelly. It lies back off the A.487 road—that's the road to Ffestiniog—and it's called Tan-y-Groes. . . . If you like I'll drop a line to the Corbetts and tell them you're coming. I'll tell them you're a friend of mine!"

"Don't bother," I said. "If I go, I'll probably get there before a letter could."

He looked at me sardonically. "Going to rush straight up there before I can get in touch with them, eh . . .? Well, you must be a glutton for punishment, that's all I can say. I assure you it'll be a pointless journey—but if I keep on saying that you'll probably think I don't want you to go!"

"Probably."

"Well, it's up to you. . . . The place is quite easy to find—you turn up a track to the left just past the fourth milestone from Dolgelly, and you'll see the white gate of the cottage about fifty yards along the track. . . ." He got up, grinning. "And I hope it keeps fine for you!"

"Thank you," I said. "If I get your story confirmed I'll come back and apologize."

"Don't worry about that, old boy. Just keep your mouth shut about my murky past until I'm safely married—that's all I ask."

I gave him a bleak nod, and left.

Chapter Sixteen

I dropped into a pub for a sandwich and a beer and sat thinking about the interview. There was nothing encouraging about it. Dancy had revealed himself more clearly than ever as a cynical and conscienceless adventurer, but that was all he had revealed. On the surface, at any rate, he couldn't have been less concerned about the murder charge. Either he was innocent or he was an incredibly cool customer—and my guess was that he was innocent. If he hadn't been in Wales over Easter I couldn't believe he'd have been so forthcoming. And if he had been in Wales he couldn't have killed Shaw.

All the same, I told myself, that alibi of his *might* have been a bluff. If in fact he had killed Shaw, and hadn't had an alibi, he'd naturally have tried to tell as convincing a story as possible in the hope that I'd drop the whole thing. Now that I'd got so far it seemed absurd not to check. Yet the thought of a solitary all-day drive to Wales and a solitary all-day drive back, with no result except finally to clinch the fact that Galloway was a murderer was almost more than I could face. Not for the first time I wished I'd left the whole thing alone, for I'd done no good to Mary or myself or anyone else.

I sat there for half an hour, trying to make up my mind what to do. If I *was* going to Wales it would mean groveling to Ames for some extra days off, because I'd no more leave due to me for a while. He'd be sure to take a dim view, particularly as I hadn't turned in any very bright stories lately. The fact was, I'd been neglecting my duties shockingly. Next thing, I'd probably find myself fired ...! With an effort, I switched my mind back to Dancy. One way or the other, I'd got to decide. Perhaps what I needed was a fresh opinion—I'd been mulling over my theory so long I couldn't judge its strength any more. I might go and see Mary. Until now I'd deliberately refrained from telling her what I'd been up to because I hadn't wanted to raise her hopes again when they'd probably only be dashed to the ground—but what I had to tell her now wouldn't raise her hopes much! I wasn't due in the office till four so I had plenty of time. I went to a phone and rang her and she'd just come in and was having lunch. I said there was something I wanted to discuss with her rather urgently and she said she'd be there all afternoon. I drove over to Kew straight away.

It was wonderful just looking at her again. It always seemed impossible she could be as lovely as I remembered her, but she always was. She seemed quite pleased to see me but there was no mistaking the gulf still there between us and I didn't have to ask her whether she'd changed her mind on fundamentals. She obviously hadn't I took my one and asked her politely how she was getting on and she said she'd fixed up a job for herself with another M.P. and would be starting at the end of the week. She asked me politely how I was getting on and I said I'd been rather busy working on the case and that there'd been a few developments—mostly, I hastened to add, disappointing ones. Then I told her everything, from the Fresher discovery onward.

I don't think I've ever seen such a transformation in anyone as I saw in Mary during the next few minutes. She'd taken it for granted I'd abandoned the case after the finding of Dancy's letter to Shaw and she was amazed and overwhelmed to learn that I'd kept on plugging away on my own. In a moment she'd thawed out completely as far as I was concerned. But that wasn't all. She was suddenly, terrifyingly hopeful again. She accepted my reconstruction as though it was a proved case. Being certain of her father's innocence, she was certain of Dancy's guilt. She said my theory must be true because we'd considered everything else and it was the only possibility left. She was enthusiastic about the way the pieces fitted together, and where they didn't—as with the newspaper cuttings—she said it was only a question of time before we found the explanation. She simply shrugged off Dancy's confident alibi. With a case like that against him, she said, he'd have to be confident, and there might be just enough truth in his story for him to think he could get away with it. Perhaps he had gone up to Wales at Easter, but the question was, *when*? Suppose he hadn't left London at midday, as he'd said—suppose he hadn't left till nine or ten at night, after the murder? And reached the Corbetts' in the morning? Or traveled up next day? *Of course* we must check.

I was horrified at her reaction. It was no good wishing now that I hadn't told her, but I did all I could to lower the temperature. I said I didn't believe the case was anything like as strong as she thought. I said I didn't think for a moment that Dancy would have expected to get away with half an alibi when he knew I'd probably check and that if we went to the cottage we'd almost certainly find he'd spent the whole weekend there and that if Mary was going to let her hopes run away with her she was in for an appalling disappointment and I didn't think I could bear to see it. But I might as well have saved my breath.

"This time," she said, "I haven't any doubts at all. . . . How soon can we start?"

We couldn't start before next day, at the earliest, because I was on duty till midnight and I still had to fix up with Ames about some extra time off. Actually I had less trouble over that than I'd expected. He grumbled a bit, but when I explained that something rather desperately personal had cropped up, he agreed to rejig the duty list and bring another man in instead. So that was all right.

We left London just after nine next morning and drove all day with the briefest of stops, taking turns at the wheel. It wasn't a journey I remember with pleasure. The roads near London were pretty congested and there was just enough light rain to mess up the windshield and make driving tricky. Later, when we got into the hills, there was some early autumn mist as well. We kept hard at it and didn't talk much. There seemed no point in further speculation about Dancy and there was too much at stake for lighthearted chatter. Once, near the end of the journey, Mary jolted me by saying, "Peter, you don't suppose he sent us all the way up here to keep us occupied while he slipped out of the country, do you?" I hadn't thought of that. It might be awkward if he did, because he was the only man who knew the whole truth—assuming he did know it. Still, flight would be a confession of guilt, and he'd probably be picked up wherever he went to. Flight would certainly be much better for us than a corroborated alibi, which was what I felt sure we were in for. Anyway, it was no good worrying about it now—we were already approaching Dolgelly. We wound our way through the last ten miles of mountains and dropped steeply into the little town just before dusk.

Finding the cottage wasn't going to be too easy in the dark, but I'd brought a good flashlight and neither of us was in the mood to put off our inquiry till the next day. We had a quick snack at a pub in Dolgelly and then pushed on along A.487 toward Ffestiniog. As I drove I worked out what I'd say to the Corbetts. They'd probably think we were quite crazy, dropping in on them in the heart of wild Wales, unannounced, in the late evening, but that couldn't be helped. I'd tell them we were friends of Dancy's, as he'd suggested; that we were on our way to the coast for a holiday and that as we were passing we'd thought we'd call in and convey Dancy's greetings. They could think what they liked. That way I could easily refer to the Easter weekend and extract my information and then we could slide gracefully out.

Having settled that, I concentrated again on the driving. The rain had stopped now but the patches of mist were troublesome and the narrow, winding road took all my attention. The country we were driving through was incredibly remote and empty. Somewhere far down on the right a torrent was raging. On the left, mountains loomed up savagely. There seemed to be no houses anywhere. There wasn't even much traffic. Presently we picked up the third milestone and I slowed down so that we shouldn't miss the fourth. We came on it suddenly round a sharp bend. Immediately beyond it I made out the track that Dancy had told me to look for. We could thank him for good directions if for nothing else. I turned the car and drove along the track for thirty or forty yards, and there was the white gate of the cottage gleaming in the headlight beam. I read the name—Tan-y-Groes. There was a light showing round the edge of the curtains in one of the downstairs rooms—the Corbetts were home. I switched off the engine and led the way up the path, shining the flashlight. The cottage seemed to face away from the track and we had to walk right round it to find the front door. I rapped on the knocker and waited. I could hear a radio playing inside. When no one came I rapped again, harder. This time a voice called out "Come in!" I turned the handle and pushed the door open. There was a small unlit hall, and immediately to the right a half-open door leading into the sitting room where the music was coming from. I tapped on the door and stuck my head inside. The room was empty. "That's odd," I said, "there's no one here." We went on in, looking around. It was a large room, lit by a single oil lamp. There was another door at the far end.

At that moment I heard a movement in the little hall behind us and a voice said sharply, "Stay where you are, both of you!"

I whipped round. I could scarcely believe my eyes—but there was no mistaking that bulky frame filling the doorway, that bald, pink head. It was Dancy—and he was pointing a gun at us.

We'd been right about him, after all!

Chapter Seventeen

He pushed the door shut behind him and stood looking at us for a moment. Then he advanced slowly into the room. He was holding the gun as though he knew how to use it. His mouth was smiling a little but his eyes were implacable. He paid hardly any attention to Mary but he was watching me all the time. The radio was blaring and he moved round and switched it off, still watching me.

"Well," he said, "so you got here at last! I was beginning to wonder if you were coming. . . . Welcome to the Corbetts'!"

I stood very still, a tight knot of fear at my stomach. It wasn't hard to guess what was going to happen next. We'd come to the end of the Galloway case in more ways than one. Obviously he intended to kill us. That was what he was here for. And there wasn't a thing we could do to stop him. Long before I could get at him he'd be able to shoot us both down. We'd nothing to bargain with, nothing to offer. There was no bluff we could hope to get away with. The most we could hope for was a little time. I wondered what he meant to do with us. He must have some tidier plan than butchering us in the sitting room.

I looked at Mary. Her eyes were blazing in a white face. I didn't need to tell her it was Dancy—she must have recognized him at once from my description. She was as tense as a coiled spring and I feared she might fling herself on him regardless of consequences. I put my hand on her arm to restrain her.

As I moved, Dancy's finger tightened on the trigger of his gun. "Keep still, Rennie!" he said. "Keep absolutely still!" He lifted the oil lamp from the table and held it so that the light fell on Mary's face. "Who's the girl?"

I didn't have a hope it would make any difference but I had to try. I said, "She's just someone I brought up for the weekend—a girl from my tennis club. We were going to have a couple of days at Barmouth. You've no quarrel with her, Dancy—she doesn't know a thing."

"You mean she *didn't* know a thing," he said. "Too bad you brought her!"

"I tell you she's just a harmless kid—she hasn't a clue about these things. She's pretty dumb, actually. If you let her go now, she won't even remember your face. . . ."

"You're wasting your breath," he said.

I tried another tack. "You'll never get away with this, Dancy. Somebody's sure to have seen you around here. When we're found . . ."

"You won't *be* found," he said. "Not where I'm going to put you."

"It still won't help you," I said desperately. "You don't realize the danger you're in. . . . Before I left London I wrote out a summary of the case against you. It's in my typewriter now. When I don't turn up, the police'll find it".

He grinned. "I used that gag in a story twenty years ago."

"This time it isn't a gag. You've got one hope and that's to clear out of the country while you can. You won't gain anything by killing us."

"I won't lose anything either because I've nothing to lose. I'll just have to take a chance on what's in your typewriter. . . . All right, that's enough talk. Let's get this over."

Suddenly Mary buried her face in my shoulder and began to sob. It was a pretty phony act to anyone who knew her. It was especially phony to me because she was digging her nails into my back, warningly. But it took Dancy in, all right. He gave her a contemptuous glance.

"I thought you said she was dumb!" he said.

"Haven't you got any heart at all, Dancy?"

"Right now," he said, "I can't afford any. Come on, break it up. . . ." He jerked the gun. "Get over to the door, both of you—we're leaving. . . ." He picked up a flashlight from the window sill. "And no tricks!—I'll be right behind you."

Still sobbing, Mary let go of me and, with her hands over her face, began to move slowly toward the door. I measured the distance between myself and Dancy. He had me covered and I knew I couldn't make it on my own. He was watching me all the time. Evidently he thought I might take a crack at him. As I stepped toward the door his eyes never left me.

That was his mistake. He ought to have been watching Mary. She was the dangerous one. She gave a little sniffle and a woebegone glance at him—and suddenly she was on him like a tigress. He swung the gun, but before he could fire it I'd reached him too. I struck the gun up and hit him hard in the face, sending him sprawling. The flashlight flew from his hand. He rolled over and over across the floor, smacked against the table, and overturned it. The oil lamp fell with a crash of splintering glass, and as he tried to get up he trod on it and the light went out. I started to go after him in the darkness, but he still had the gun and he fired twice as I fumbled my way toward him. The bullets missed me, but not by much. It suddenly seemed stupid to try and argue with a gun when all we wanted was to get away. I called, "Mary, where are you?" and ducked as Dancy fired again. I could hear him lumbering about unsteadily—that blow of mine seemed to have shaken him. Then I felt Mary beside me. "The door!" I whispered. Together we groped our way toward it as another bullet ripped into the wall. In a moment Mary had found the latch and we were through the door and opening the outer one.

"Quick!—the car!" I said. We turned and raced round the corner of the cottage, hoping for a clean getaway. But we were too late. Dancy must have gone out by the other, nearer door, for he was already on the rutted track, between us and the car. I could see his head against the windshield. As we jerked to a stop he fired twice, and again the shots came dangerously close. I grabbed Mary's arm and swung her round and we retreated behind the cottage. I pulled out my flashlight and flashed it around and there was a stream and a little bridge, which we crossed. As long as we kept away from that gun it didn't matter which way we went. A path took us through some bushes and we suddenly found ourselves out on the track again, but higher up. We turned to the left, in the opposite direction from the road. I could hear Dancy running—he'd heard us and was coming after us. We broke into a run ourselves. The surface was uneven and several times we stumbled, but I daren't use the flashlight in the open. Anyway, we were gaining ground—Dancy hadn't the build for running up mountains. He'd never catch us now. After a bit we slowed down. Mary was breathless, but mostly from excitement. "Peter," she gasped, "we've *done* it! Oh, Peter . . .!"

We jogged on for a hundred yards or so. The track had leveled out and seemed to be entering a sort of gully. It was too dark to see anything clearly but I had the impression of high banks on both sides. Presently we rounded a bend and I switched the flashlight on again. As I'd thought, we were in a cutting. The banks on either side were almost perpendicular. I felt a tremor of anxiety, but with Dancy still pounding along behind us we had no choice but to go on. We continued for another fifty yards. Then, suddenly, the track came to an end. And what an end! As I shone the flashlight around I saw that on each side of us there was an unscalable rock face. Ahead, there was another wall of rock. It was broken by a single opening, dark and forbidding—a rectangle eight or nine feet wide and a little over six feet high. We were at the entrance to some old mine.

It was a grim moment. If we entered the mine we might well find ourselves in a trap. Once Dancy caught up with us in a confined space we'd be helpless against his gun. But we had to go on, or back—there was no other way. And Dancy was coming up fast. If we turned we'd have to face the gun at once. It was a choice of evils—and the mine seemed the lesser evil. Once inside, we might be able to give him the slip. There might be more than one passage. There might be places where we could hide. And at least we had a good flashlight. We plunged in. After we'd gone a little way we stopped to listen. There wasn't much doubt that Dancy would follow us in, but I wanted to make sure. He seemed to have paused by the entrance. Suddenly I caught a sinister sound. He was reloading his gun. After a moment I heard cautious steps. He was coming in for the kill. We didn't wait any longer.

The tunnel drove straight into the mountain. The floor was level, and unobstructed except for an occasional bit of crumbling rail. The walls and roof were of rough-hewn rock, solid as the mountain itself. Dancy was the only hazard. I fell into a routine of flashing the light at frequent intervals, but only for a split second at a time, because of the gun. Between the flashes we walked in darkness. We had no trouble keeping ahead for Dancy hadn't had time to recover his own flashlight and now that he was in the tunnel he wasn't attempting to hurry. Every few yards he stopped and struck a match, which made it easy for us to judge his progress. I thought he was probably afraid of an ambush, but he needn't have worried for the walls were regular on both sides and offered no cover at all.

We pushed on for a hundred yards or so, maintaining our lead and looking all the time for someplace that would give us a chance to maneuver. Then the character of the tunnel began to change. We seemed to have come through the rock into some softer stuff and everything was beginning to get very wet. Pit props and timber balks had been used to shore up the walls and roof, and water was seeping down between them, red and muddy from the earth it had flowed through. On our faces and necks, the drips felt icy cold. The air had become dank and foul-smelling. Many of the pit props were rotten and in some places there'd been slight falls where the timber had broken away. Probably, I thought, this was an old gold mine, in which case it might have been derelict for fifty years or more. I didn't like the look of things at all, now, and I could tell from Mary's tight grip on my hand that she didn't, either. But Dancy was still coming on. Every few seconds a tiny glimmer broke the darkness as he struck another match. There was nothing for it but to keep going. At least he was no longer taking pot shots at us, which was some consolation. The place was unnerving enough without that.

I was still hoping the passage would divide—and finally it did.

As I flashed the light for a routine check, Mary suddenly gave a cry and pointed to an opening on the right. It was a tunnel of the same size, going off at an angle of about sixty degrees. It looked in better shape than the one we were in and we swung into it without slowing down. I switched the flashlight off before we turned and for fifty yards we moved on tiptoe. Then we stopped to listen again. It was a tense moment, for there was an even chance now that we might shake Dancy off. If he took the other passage we could be safely out of the mine in ten minutes. We waited, scarcely daring to breathe. We heard him reach the fork and stop. A match scraped and a light flared. He seemed to be hesitating. When the match flickered out, he struck another one at once. He hadn't done that before. He seemed to be bending down. Suddenly I knew that it hadn't been an even chance after all. He was looking for our footmarks in the wet ground. Evidently he found them, for very soon he took up the trail again at the same unhurried pace.

From that moment everything seemed to go against us. I'd even been wrong about the right-hand fork being in better shape than the other one. It had started off better, but now it was deteriorating fast. It was terribly wet, and in places we had to splash ankle-deep through pools of mud and water. Many of the props were so rotten that they were bulging under the weight of earth. Some had come away altogether. At one spot, a section of wall had caved right in, forming a mound of mud and props halfway across the passage. If conditions got any worse we'd be in real trouble. I wondered how much further the tunnel went into the mountain. Somewhere, surely, there must be workings. That was what we needed now to give us a chance—an underground quarry with plenty of room. . . . Then, as I pressed the flashlight button for another quick check, I stopped bothering about what lay ahead. For us, nothing lay ahead—except rubble. The roof had fallen in and the way was blocked.

Now we were really in a trap. For a moment I could see no ray of hope at all. If Dancy approached us with caution, using plenty of matches, he'd be able to shoot us long before we could do anything about him. We'd be sitting birds. If only there'd been a bit of cover . . .! Suddenly I thought of the mound of mud where the wall had caved in. It wasn't much of a place for an ambush but it would be better than nothing and it was only a few yards away. I grabbed Mary's arm and we raced back. In a matter of seconds we'd reached the mound and flung ourselves down behind it in the soft mud. Dancy was still hidden by a curve in the tunnel. I switched on the flashlight for a quick reconnaissance. It wasn't a very healthy spot—the roof timbers were bad, as well as the wall. Several of them had broken away at one end and were drooping down. But we were in no position to be choosy. I snapped off the light. Mary said, "What are you going to do?" She was trembling a little. I said, "I'll have to try and rush him—it's the only way now." She pressed close against me. "Be as careful as you can," she said. I squeezed her hand, and looked out over the top of the mound. Dancy was just coming round the bend, thirty yards away. He was moving more slowly and carefully than ever and striking far more matches. It was just as though he knew about the mound. I suddenly wondered if he'd been in the mine before. He might have been. He might have known all the time that the passage was blocked ahead. That would account for his leisurely pursuit. He might even have planned to kill us here in the first place. If so, we'd certainly made it easy for him!

It was a nerve-racking wait in the cold, clammy darkness. He was coming on at a snail's pace. Matches flickered and died. Slowly, very slowly, the gap narrowed. He must be pretty close now, I thought—not more than twenty feet. I braced myself. The mud wouldn't make much of a springboard but it was all I had. I could hear him advancing again, very warily. I felt sure he knew about the mound. Anyway, he must have seen it by now. He'd strike one more match, I thought, before he reached it. His gun would be at the ready. I'd have to rush him as the light went out. Timing would be everything. I'd have to try and make it in one bound. I waited tensely. A match scraped. The light was so close I daren't even raise my head. The match seemed to burn for hours! As it went out I hurled myself forward. At the same instant, Dancy fired. The noise was fiendish in the narrow passage—but he missed again. I plunged toward him. My feet slid wildly in the mud. Suddenly I was falling! I grabbed for the roof to steady myself. Whatever I grabbed was loose and came away in my hand. An avalanche of earth started to pour down on me. There was a deep rumbling noise, as though the whole mountain was splitting in two. I scrambled back, and as I did so the roof in front of me collapsed with a great roar. I called, "Mary, where are you?" flashing the light. Then something hit me and everything went black.

Chapter Eighteen

I came round to find Mary kneeling beside me. She'd got the flashlight and was shining it down on me. "Peter!" she was saying in an agitated voice. "Peter, are you all right?"

I struggled into a sitting position. We were on the very edge of the debris. I moved my arms and legs and felt my head. I had a cut over my right temple but I didn't seem to have suffered any serious damage. "Yes," I said, "I'm all right. . . . How long have I been out?"

"Not long—only a couple of minutes."

"Are *you* all right?"

"Yes, I got out of the way just in time. . . . Peter, we're shut in!"

I heaved myself up and took the flashlight from her and shone it on the rubble. It was a frightening sight. A mass of earth and stones and props had completely closed the passage where the mound of mud had been. We were imprisoned now between two falls, in a stretch of tunnel scarcely twenty feet long. We were safe from Dancy's bullets, but it didn't look as though our prospects of survival had improved.

Mary said, "How long do you think the air will last?"

"Probably longer than the flashlight battery," I said. "Come on, let's have a look round while we can."

Very cautiously, we picked our way over the outer rubble and approached the new fall. It was quite impossible to tell how far the block extended. I listened, but I couldn't hear anything from the other side. I said, "I wonder what happened to Dancy?"

"I think he got away," Mary said. "I heard him give a shout as the roof collapsed, but it seemed to come from a long way off. I think he must have scrambled back when you did."

I nodded, and had another look at the debris. Everything was terribly loose and precarious. When I tried to pull some of the stuff away, more earth came down and filled the gap at once. If we attempted to do any excavating there, the chances were we'd start another fall and bring the rest of the roof down on top of us.

I crossed to the other block and took a closer look at that. It was a much older one and the earth and props were well compacted. Once again, since the tunnel was completely closed, there was no means of telling how far the block went—but it was certainly in a less dangerous state.

"We might be able to burrow through here," I said.

"I'm ready. . . . Peter, we've *got* to get out now. We've simply got to!"

"We don't know what's on the other side."

"We'll have to take a chance on that. . . . Come on, let's get started."

Very carefully, I began to pull away the earth at the bottom left-hand corner of the fall. It was moist, and by digging my fingers deep into it I was able to drag it away in handfuls. The props at the side of the fall still seemed to be intact. I worked inward from them, gradually scooping out a triangular hole about two feet high at the side and eighteen inches along the bottom. As I pushed the loose earth back, Mary moved it into the tunnel, out of the way. Most of the time we worked in darkness, keeping the torch for examining the hole at intervals. We made good progress at first, burrowing away with desperate intensity, but it was hard on the hands and I didn't think we'd get far without some sort of tool. In the end Mary took over while I searched around for something to dig with. Most of the small bits of timber lying around were too rotten to be any use, but presently I found a couple of flattish stones in the debris round the other fall. After that we got on faster.

As we continued to dig, conditions in the hole grew steadily more uncomfortable. The work at the face was terribly exhausting because of the cramped position, and by the time we'd reached a depth of five feet I was having to take frequent rests. To speed things up we organized a system of shifts with ten minutes on and ten minutes off, whoever was shoveling the earth back from the entrance acting as timekeeper. It worked well and we soon developed a smooth rhythm. When we changed over we refreshed ourselves by letting a few drops of water trickle into our mouths from the streaming tunnel roof. It wasn't much of a restorative but it was better than nothing.

At six feet I came across an obstacle—a broken roof balk wedged slap across the hole. It was too close to the hard floor to burrow under so I started to scoop the earth away above it. I'd hardly begun when, without any warning, a weight came down on my head and shoulders, forcing my face into the ground. I gave a muffled yell and flailed wildly with my feet, which was all I could do. With my arms pinned in front of me, it was impossible to wriggle back. The earth seemed to be closing in—I could scarcely breathe. The blood pounded in my head. This, I thought, is it! Then I felt Mary's hands gripping my ankles and a succession of increasingly desperate tugs that finally drew me back, inch by inch, till I could use my arms once more. I struggled out, spitting earth and feeling pretty shaken.

"God," I said, "that was a near thing!"

Mary's face was stiff with fright. "You were so heavy I didn't think I'd be able to move you. . . . What happened?"

"A bit of the roof fell."

"Is it bad?"

"It felt pretty bad."

"Shall I take over?"

"No, I'll go back and have a look, first."

I rested a few moments and then went in again with the flashlight to see what the damage was. Actually, it was nothing like as bad as I'd feared. The fall had been a minor one and I soon had the rubble cleared away. It had come from under another jammed beam and as long as that held I didn't think there'd be another fall in the same spot. I scooped a space between the balks of timber, just large enough to get through, and continued to pass the loose stuff back to Mary. Presently we resumed our shifts.

There were no more serious incidents, but we seemed as far as ever from a breakthrough. By now we'd been digging for over two hours—my watch showed nearly midnight—and we were so tired that our actions were becoming mechanical. Around one o'clock we gave up changing places—the hole had grown so deep that we both had to work inside it anyway, so there seemed no point in switching over. We didn't talk much, except to report progress or trouble. Mostly there was nothing to report at all—we just kept on digging and shifting the earth. The way Mary stuck at it, dogged and uncomplaining, was incredible. I'd never admired her indomitable spirit more.

By two o'clock we'd penetrated more than twelve feet and we still hadn't got anywhere. We were both utterly whacked and I was beginning to think we'd had it. We took another short rest out in the tunnel, leaning back against the wall to ease our cramped muscles. The air wasn't as good as it had been and my head felt thick and heavy. I could easily have given up and drowsed away into a stupor, but Mary roused me and said we must keep going while we could. We crawled back into the hole and I started to scrape away at the face once more. Most of the stuff I'd been hacking out lately had been soft wet clay, but now I'd come to looser stuff again and I was beginning to fear another fall. I dug away cautiously with my flat stone—and suddenly it went through! A draft of cold air blew around my face. I widened the gap and shone the flashlight through it—and there, beyond a pile of rubble, I could see the passage again, intact.

I twisted my head round and called excitedly to Mary that we'd made it. Then, with infinite care, I pushed out the earth ahead of me until there was enough room for my shoulders to pass through. A moment later I'd wriggled out. I flashed the light back and called to Mary to come. I held my breath as she came elbowing her way through the loose stuff at the end, but she managed it all right. In a few seconds she was standing beside me.

It was indescribably wonderful to be able to move freely

again—but we still hardly dared to hope. This tunnel could easily come to an abrupt end and that would be the end of us too. There might be another roof fall ahead, and neither of us had the strength to do any more burrowing. Indeed, we were so exhausted we could scarcely walk. We set off at a slow, stumbling pace, supporting each other. We'd covered only fifty yards when the tunnel forked again. It didn't seem to matter much which fork we took. There'd been so many twists since we'd entered the mine that we no longer had the slightest sense of direction. The main thing, obviously, was to keep bearing the same way all the time—then, at least, we shouldn't lose ourselves entirely and we might be able to work our way round to the entrance again. We chose the left fork and staggered on. After a while we came to yet another fork, and once more we turned left. Almost at once the condition of the passage began to deteriorate. It was nearly as wet as the bit where we'd been trapped. Suddenly I stumbled over something—a loose piece of wood. I switched on the now feeble flashlight and peered ahead. It was what I'd most feared! Immediately in front of us there'd been another fall, and once more the passage was blocked.

I put my arms round Mary and held her close. The blow was all the worse because at last we'd seemed to be making progress. Now, at the limit of endurance, the thought of retracing our steps and trying to explore the other turnings with a failing light was almost more than we could contemplate. For a moment we stood in despairing silence, clinging to each other. Then the silence was suddenly broken. From just ahead there came a low groan!

I could hardly believe it. I took a step forward and held the flashlight close to the ground. At first I could see nothing but debris. Then, as I moved the torch, I saw a man's head. It was Dancy. He was lying on his back at the edge of the rubble, with only his head and shoulders visible. His legs and torso were firmly held by a roof prop and a great heap of earth.

Even then, I didn't realize what had happened—not at first. I thought that Dancy must have been caught by a second fall on his way out and that now we were all trapped together. It was Mary who hit on the truth—that this was the original fall, and that we'd worked round to the back of it. That last fork where we'd turned left was the one where, on first entering the mine, we'd turned right. We were only a few hundred yards from the entrance. We were free!

Chapter Nineteen

Dancy was conscious, and he kept on groaning, but there was almost nothing we could do for him on our own. He was so firmly held that there wasn't a chance of extricating him and anyway the roof above him looked as though a touch would bring it down. If he was to be got out alive, a properly equipped rescue party was the only thing. I gave him a few drops of water and told him we'd send help, and we left him.

The rectangle of pale dawn light at the exit from the mine was the most welcome sight I'd ever seen. Outside, we stopped for a moment to look at each other, exchanging wan smiles of incredulous relief, which was about the sharpest emotion either of us was capable of feeling just then. We were both pretty well all in. Mary's appearance was terrifying, and mine, I knew, was no better. From head to foot we were completely caked in mud. Our best plan, I thought, was to go straight to the police, who were used to shocks. Somehow we succeeded in dragging ourselves to the car and by concentrating fiercely I managed to keep it on the road for the four miles to Dolgelly.

There was a gaunt Welsh sergeant in charge of the station. He gaped at us when we staggered in, but once he'd grasped the situation and realized that a man was still trapped in the mine he acted quickly. While the rescue party was being mobilized we told him enough of the background story to make sure that a close eye would be kept on Dancy pending inquiries. A constable fixed us up with some cups of sweet tea and I drew a sketch map showing where Dancy would be found. Then Mary was put in the care of the sergeant's wife at a cottage a few doors away and I was given a bed in a cell. For the next few hours that was all I wanted.

I woke just before noon, refreshed and ravenously hungry. Mary, I learned, was already up. Someone got my case from the car and I gave myself as thorough a clean-up as I could manage. Then I walked round to the cottage, where the kindly sergeant's wife had insisted on preparing lunch for us. Mary had transformed herself and looked more than presentable. She was in such high spirits that she could scarcely contain herself. What she wanted to do, of course, was rush straight back to town and get the wonderful news to her father as quickly as she could, but we had a few things to attend to first. After we'd eaten we went back to the station and had a conference with the Chief Constable and the local C.I.D. people. Dancy, we learned, had been safely brought out of the mine and was now in hospital—fairly battered, but in no danger. We went through our whole story in great detail and it took most of the afternoon. Then we drove back to London.

For several days after that, things were pretty hectic. It had never occurred to me that as a result of the Dancy business I might get the newspaper story of the year—I'd never been hopeful enough of the outcome—but I'd certainly got it, and now, with an undivided mind, I could set about being a decent reporter again. Apart from getting the story into print there were meetings with high-ups at the Yard and the Home Office that Mary and I had to attend. Things were obviously going to take a bit of sorting out, but Mary and her father had seen the lawyers, and machinery was being set in motion to get him out of prison, by one means or another, at the earliest possible moment. It seemed certain, the lawyers said, that he'd be given a "free pardon" as soon as the position had been fully investigated. Mary was indignant at the phrase, but not at anything else. It was wonderful to see her happy again—and in her happiness I fully shared. With luck, I hoped to go on sharing it for a long time!

It was some days before Dancy was sufficiently recovered from his injuries to be questioned by the police—and then he wouldn't talk.

But they kept plugging away at him, pointing out that after what he'd tried to do to us he hadn't a leg to stand on, and in the end they got some sort of statement out of him. That, together with what we knew from other sources and what we could reasonably surmise, made it possible to fill in most of the remaining gaps in the case.

It had all started, apparently, with a discovery that Shaw had made two years before—a discovery which until now we hadn't known about, and which explained one of the things that had been puzzling me—why Shaw had bothered so much about Fresher in the first place. It seemed that during his research work for his "200 detective plots" monograph he'd come across a story which had greatly intrigued him. It had been a recently published book by Richard Dancy, and the reason for Shaw's interest had been that it had at once reminded him of another and much older story in his collection—*The Black Hat*, by Grant Fresher. He'd reread *The Black Hat* and had decided that Dancy had lifted Fresher's old plot. Partly because he'd been genuinely interested and partly because he'd hoped it might be worth a bit to him to draw Fresher's attention to the plagiarism, he'd gone to see Fresher's publishers to find out who Fresher was. He'd there learned about Fresher's unsavory past and been given Fresher's photograph. By now it had already crossed his mind that the two men might be one and the same, and out of curiosity he'd called on Dancy and confirmed his suspicion. Dancy had been annoyed at having his former identity uncovered by a prying stranger, but he hadn't been particularly worried. As he'd merely rehashed a twenty-year-old plot of his own, there'd been no question of plagiarism and at that time there'd been no hint of blackmail. Indeed, there hadn't been any scope for it. Dancy had been openly cynical about his past record and in any case had appeared not to have much money. He'd not yet met Lavinia Hewitt.

What had actually started Shaw on his complicated frame-up plan could only be a matter of speculation, but the supposition was that he'd probably looked in on Galloway's television interview. He'd heard Galloway say that he hadn't got a plot; he'd known that Galloway's plots often made big money; and the possibilities of lucrative plagiarism had already been in his mind. The fact that his own ambition to make money out of writing had been constantly thwarted might well have given him an impetus. Anyhow, he'd plunged with enthusiasm into his tortuous plan.

Dancy had never been privy to Shaw's scheme. Shaw had gone ahead on his own, clearing his first and worst hurdle when he'd submitted a typescript to Galloway and got it back unopened, and then preparing to cook up various bits of evidence which would later support his claim. The most important of these was to be a corroboratory letter from Dancy. Shaw's idea had been that after the publication of Galloway's story he'd take his own version of it to Dancy, tell him that Galloway had stolen his plot, explain that in order to make his legitimate claim effective he needed a predated letter from Dancy, and offer a small part of the proceeds of his claim as a bribe.

Soon after the publication of Galloway's book, Shaw had gone to Dancy with his tale. Dancy had not only not believed in Shaw's claim—he hadn't thought much of its prospects, either, and he hadn't been willing to write the letter. Shaw had persisted—all the more so because by now there was a new factor in the situation—Lavinia Hewitt. Shaw had met her at Dancy's on this second visit and had at once suspected that there might be money involved. He'd checked on Lavinia, as I'd done, and had discovered what was at stake. He'd now had a real hold on Dancy, whose wooing of Lavinia at that time had been in an early and delicate stage. However, he'd played his cards carefully and kept his trump back. At a third meeting he'd again asked for a letter, this time producing various bits of faked evidence as confirmation of the fact that he was the original author of the disputed plot. They'd included not merely the underwater books and the notebook and the draft chapter but also the newspaper cuttings. Just how Shaw had come by those cuttings was still a matter of conjecture, but a possible explanation emerged as a result of police inquiries at Mrs. Green's. It seemed that for more than a year before his death, Shaw had had a great stack of old newspapers in his room which he'd told his sister he wanted to keep. The police theory was that immediately on conceiving his frame-up plot, he'd collected up all the newspapers he could lay his hands on, some of them already several weeks old, and put them away in cold storage. Then, when Galloway's book had been published and he'd discovered its subject, he'd gone through his newspapers and managed to find cuttings that bore on the underwater theme. Since Galloway's stories had almost always dealt with matters of topical interest, the expectation of finding newspaper coverage would have been reasonable. In view of the little man's foresight in other directions, it seemed a very feasible explanation.

The weight of evidence put before Dancy must have been impressive, but he'd still hesitated. He hadn't trusted Shaw and he hadn't been convinced. He'd held back not from any scruple, but because he hadn't wanted to risk getting into any fresh trouble with the law at a time when his own prospects had been bright. Shaw, for his part, had maintained that there was no possibility of trouble—that Galloway, with all the evidence arrayed against him, would never dare to take the matter to court and would have no alternative but to settle up quietly in the very near future. If Dancy would write the letter, he'd said, he could have twenty-five per cent of the expected proceeds—and probably in a matter of days. Dancy had been in acute need of ready cash at the time, being eager to give Lavinia the impression that he was a man of means and not a fortune hunter. In the end he'd fallen for the bribe and agreed to write the letter. Shaw's blackmail trump hadn't been needed.

Almost immediately after Shaw had got his letter, Arthur Blundell had died. Whether Shaw had actually collected autographs at the Mystery Guild exhibition in the hope that he might be able to use one of them for his plot, or whether he'd merely garnered them out of interest and remembered them on reading of Blundell's death and decided to turn Blundell's to account, was never really cleared up. Whatever the fact, Shaw had certainly realized that a well-faked letter from Blundell would be much safer for his purpose than the one he'd got from Dancy. Blundell was dead and couldn't be questioned. Dancy could, and Dancy had a police record, which might be discovered if anything went wrong. The sudden opportunity had been too good to pass up. Shaw had therefore gone to considerable trouble and taken some risks to perfect the Blundell forgery. Once it was done, he'd felt completely secure. He'd shown it to Dancy, and coolly explained that he'd had it all the time and had only wanted Dancy's letter as additional confirmation, and said it probably wouldn't be necessary for him to use Dancy's letter now, though he'd still pay for it. Dancy had been completely foxed by the new development. He'd still had the feeling that Shaw was somehow pulling a fast one, but he hadn't had a notion how.

Then had come the negotiations with Galloway. For Shaw, they'd been a sharp disappointment. Instead of coming to terms like a reasonable man, Galloway had dug in his heels and refused to pay. By now Shaw had gone much too far with his accusations to be able to withdraw them, even if he'd wanted to. Galloway was putting the matter into the hands of his solicitors and was going to fight the thing through. That meant that Shaw had to fight, too. But with what? A protracted lawsuit might run into thousands. At that point Shaw had gone back to Dancy, in a desperate and panicky state of mind. He'd told Dancy that things had gone wrong and that they'd have to raise a fighting fund if they were to get the compensation they'd hoped for. Dancy had told him to go to hell. Shaw had then produced his trump. Dancy had better get the money out of his rich fiancee, he'd said, or she'd learn about the Fresher affair and he wouldn't have a fiancée any longer. There'd been a savage row. Dancy had said that if he tried to borrow money from Lavinia it would probably be the end anyway. Shaw had said he'd better think up some plausible story and get round her—or else! It was up to him. Meanwhile Shaw would go and see Galloway on his boat that evening and make one more attempt to get him to see reason.

Dancy had brooded darkly over the situation after Shaw had left. By now he'd come to fear and hate Shaw, whom he regarded as a cunning and dangerous little rat. He'd decided there was only one way he could safeguard his position with Lavinia—he'd have to dispose of the rat. Shaw's visit to Galloway's boat would provide the perfect opportunity. But there'd been one serious snag. As it happened, Dancy had invited Lavinia to dine with him in town that Easter Saturday evening. In order to carry out his program, he'd been forced to put her off. He'd been reluctant to give illness as an excuse because she'd be bound to make fussy inquiries afterward and if he'd been as ill as all that he'd hardly have left his flat. In the end he'd telephoned her, full of apologies, and said that a friend of his, a fellow named Jack Reed, had just had a bad car smash, and Reed's family had asked him to rally round. Lavinia had accepted that and they'd made a fresh date for after Easter. Dancy had then driven to Kingston, stuck a hammer in his pocket from the car tool kit, walked along the towpath at dusk, and awaited his chance. He'd overheard the quarrel from a hiding place behind some bushes and later had followed Shaw along the towpath and killed him.

After that, everything had gone smoothly for Dancy. His courting had prospered. Galloway, most conveniently, had been convicted of the murder. The case had been satisfactorily closed. Then I'd arrived on the scene and started to rake up the past. Dancy had appeared genuinely fascinated by my reconstruction of the Shaw frame-up plan because it had in fact all been new to him. At that crucial meeting he'd also realized his danger. He'd known, what I couldn't know, that if the police ever got around to making a check on how he'd spent that fatal Easter Saturday evening, he'd be sunk. He couldn't hope to get away with the usual vague kind of answer—that he'd been at the pictures or out for a stroll—because a single question to Lavinia might well uncover the fact that he'd canceled a date, and the police would want to know why. And his friend Jack Reed had been an imaginary friend who'd had an imaginary accident. So when, after making out a pretty impressive case, I'd raised the question of where he'd been at the time of the murder, he'd decided that the only safe thing was to get rid of me, too. Pretending to be worried solely about his standing with Lavinia, he'd quickly satisfied himself that I hadn't mentioned my suspicions to anyone else. Then he'd told me about the cottage in Wales. He hadn't been there at Easter, but he had been there several times before and he knew the Corbetts well. What was more, he knew the cottage was empty at that moment, because the letter he'd had from the Corbetts a fortnight earlier had come from Madeira and had mentioned that they'd be abroad for a month. Up there in the lonely mountains he could dispose of me without any risk of discovery. After I'd left him he'd driven straight up there, parked his car in a Dolgelly car park, walked in darkness to the cottage, and passed an anxious twenty-four hours waiting for me. Mary had been an unexpected complication, but he'd had no choice but to take her in his stride. His intention had been to march us at pistol point to the old mine, which he'd reconnoitered the previous day, and kill us there, and leave us deep inside where we'd never be found. Afterward, he'd intended to drive my car back to London, leave it near my flat, return by train to Dolgelly to collect his own car, and then quietly take up the threads of his life again.

Well, it had nearly worked!

www.ingramcontent.com/pod-product-compliance
Ingram Content Group UK Ltd.
Pitfield, Milton Keynes, MK11 3LW, UK
UKHW040105010325
455690UK00002B/15